100 Days of

JJ

A Unique Love Story

Book 2

Brian J Logsdon

Cover images by DALL-E.

ISBN- 9798327806887

DEDICATION

To Jimmy,
Who Went "All In."

ACKNOWLEDGMENTS

I've been writing about what I believe for most of my life. Those beliefs have changed for most of my life!

What remains are a few fundamental belief systems that align with those of my parents, siblings, and now, most especially, my partner in life.

I have also read many, many authors and gleaned some facets from each of them. I couldn't begin to list them all.

My Mom is smiling at me and reminding me what a good boy I am to remember to thank those from whom we learn…

My Dad is smiling at me for being a responsible human being.

101 JJ'S ANSWER

"It's the stuff of dreams
The world's not what it might seem
Shining at its seams."

Jimmy saw it again and jerked his head to the left, but it was gone before he could bring it into focus. 'The world's shining at the seams again,' he thought. He'd seen it before, like auras around things or energy leaking from the shapes in the world. He mostly shook his head to clear it, having given himself the explanation that 'forms are made of energy, and the eyes can't always define the form of things quickly.' That idea typically satisfied the mind, allowing it to move on without a clear definition. Other times, he used 'This world's not intended to be understood' or 'Life is just a game to be played out.' All the "answers" left him with a nagging doubt that he knew anything at all about "reality."

'Just keep moving,' he thought. 'The Universe loves movement.' This, at least, he could verify just by sitting in one place too long and allowing his body to atrophy. 'Or is it the mind that stagnates, requiring extra energy to get the body moving again?' Either way, ibuprofen seemed to help. 'Although that is most likely an idea in the mind, too.'

"Jenny." Jimmy liked the way her name rolled off his tongue. "Jenny, do you think we'll ever know what's really going on?"
"Well, Jimmy, you'll have to be more specific if you really want an

4

answer." She loved to tease him, and he seemed to love being teased.

"Just in general, Jenny. Where does the time go when we fall asleep and the world drifts away? Or even how is it that we wake up to another day and most things are still the same? Both are equally impossible to answer, it seems."

"Well, Jimmy, maybe we're not supposed to know the answers to those questions. It might take all the fun out of it!"

"The 'not knowing' does keep things interesting, Jenny!"

"You know it, Jimmy!" They laughed together at that, maybe because there were no answers.

"I can't explain it, Jenny, but somehow I love this life together more and more each day."

"Me, too, Jimmy. And I don't think it's explainable. Love just 'is,' is all." She leaned into him and kissed him.

"Mmmm, Mmmm, Jenny!" Jimmy laughed and smacked his lips. "Life really IS tasty with you!"

"That's the peanuts I just ate!"

"Ah, yes. That's not playing fair, Girlfriend. You know how much I love peanut butter!"

"I didn't know there were rules, Jimmy." Jenny grinned mischievously.

"OK, Baby, no rules." Jimmy grinned at her. "And no explanation needed. I'll just keep on loving you."

"Now that IS tasty, Boyfriend!"

"There is only This,
whatever This is."

102 JJ'S ADVENTURE

"We are the creators of our own world."

Jimmy knew that he didn't need to remodel the basement. It was just one of many possible futures for the space. He had thought about putting in some rolling cabinets like the ones in the garage. He had thought about doing nothing with it, letting the accumulated "stuff" sit on the shelves for someone else to sort through and dispose of. Yet now he was in the middle of it, enjoying the creativity of making a new space, both functional and fun, a sort of legacy to complete the spaces that the guy who initially "flipped" the house hadn't finished.

"Always leave a place better than you found it." Did Dad say that? It seemed like a good way to live. At any rate, Jimmy was carrying on the "time-honored tradition" of changing his environment to make it "better."

Jimmy had learned many things working in construction. One of them was, "If you want a thing done right, do it yourself." Though somewhat egocentric, this saying, like many others, was true some of the time. Another was, "If you want to get a thing done, hire someone to do it."

Jimmy had used that line, too. He had even combined the two by supervising those he had hired. Maybe the "best of both worlds?"

One of the most fun things in life for Jimmy was taking what he thought he knew and trying it out "in the real world." Nothing was truly "known" unless it could be "proven," right? And the ego certainly liked to be "right."

Jimmy framed and split wood, wired and popped breakers, drilled and sawed and nailed, planned and executed, enjoying every bit of creation's trials. Not to mention that the Universe loved movement, and he was doing plenty of that! He went to bed a little sore and a little fulfilled every night. "And on the seventh day, He rested."

"Jenny, do you think I'll get done in time?" Jimmy liked bouncing things off Jenny - she always "told it to him straight."

"Well, Jimmy, you're definitely doing things 'in time,' but 'on time' is harder to tell. Is there a deadline?"

"Jenny, you reflect me so well." He shook his head. "I'm just looking for some encouragement, I guess."

"You're doing a great job, Jimmy! I love watching you do your 'manly things.' It's interesting and sometimes amusing. Especially when you talk to yourself."

"I'm just checking in with the Universe to see if I'm forgetting something."

"And...?" Jenny asked.

"Yes and no. There are things I could have done differently, but overall, the plan is still coming together, and when it's done, it will allow for the greatest possibilities of future utility."

"Whatever you just said sounded good to me, Jimmy! So, the Universe really IS on your side." Jenny said it as fact, not a question.

"You know it!" Jimmy quipped. "And so do I! At least, most of the time." Jimmy found that being truthful made him the happiest. He knew that things could be shaped by half-truths, too, but that didn't feel as good.

"Now, Jenny, if I can find just enough time to get this done before we get busy in spring and summer! You know we'll want to get out camping as soon as possible!"

"I'm sure we'll be planning our next adventure soon, Jimmy. And I can hardly wait!"

"Everything is an adventure
waiting to happen."

103 JJ'S NOTION

"Nothing ventured.
Nothing gained."

Jimmy seemed to see things differently. Sometimes, he felt as if that made him all alone in a world of his own, following some strange destiny. It really didn't matter much what he did or didn't do, sort of like Bill Murray in Groundhog Day. Maybe that's why he liked that movie - it looked a lot like his own. He wondered if the answer really was to truly love, and then every day would be different again!

Then Jenny showed up.

Every day was different and exquisitely the same! There was nothing that he wanted to change and everything to rearrange, making love the primary act on the stage.

"Jenny, Darling?"
"Jimmy, Daring One?"
"Just checking that you were awake. I don't really need anything."
"All I need is this, Jimmy."
"I'm with you on that, Girlfriend!"
"Then come closer and hold me tight."
"Holding on with all my might!"
"What day is it, Jimmy?"
"Today."

"Now is the time..."

104 JJ'S RISE

"Letting go,
we have it All."

Jimmy wasn't sure how anything happened anymore. Life had surprised him so many times that he had finally "learned his lesson" - he wasn't in control of any of it. It hadn't been easy to learn—or maybe "unlearn" better described it - his mind traveled deeply entrenched paths, only peering over the edge to see if the war was still going on. It wasn't likely to jump up and run towards its inevitable "death."

"Only the time it takes is voluntary." Jimmy had read something like that somewhere - it didn't matter where anymore - and he knew that it was true - as accurate as anything else, that is. Somewhere in the "Letting go of the need to know," ideas of cause and effect, blame and names, and responsibility games had fallen away with a grin. No one loses; no one wins. There's just this Flow we're in.

If there's a prompting to turn left, by all means, turn left! An inkling of joy, you say. Definitely, head that way! Heading towards the Light surely makes this life seem bright. Love is always right.

"Jenny," Jimmy said her name like it was his own. "Jenny, I think the Universe really does love movement."

"Jimmy, does that mean we have to get out of bed?"

"Not right now, thank God, Jenny!"

"Whew! You had me worried for a second!" Jenny laughed, knowing that there was never anything to worry about.

Jimmy laughed with her. Jenny had become his Muse for everything good in life, and his love for her had become boundless -

with no fear or worry, there were no limits.

"You're SO fun, Girlfriend! You know exactly what I mean." Jenny did know. Jimmy had dreamed it that way, and by never holding anything back, he purposefully maintained the lack of separation. Acknowledging the unity of their relationship confirmed the "Unity Consciousness" of the Universe in which they lived.

"Amen, Jimmy."

Jimmy knew that Jenny would say that.

"What I was thinking of is that we seem to have moved from an early stage of love, when we shared spit, dinners, and dance, to a 'next level' of living together and noticing the seamless ways in which love can grow just by letting go of ego, to this moment, in which the entire universe revolves around our love."

"Whew, again, Jimmy! But you're right - there has been a seeming progression in our intimacy - or 'sharing spit,' as you so eloquently put it - that has brought us to this 'Now,' when there really isn't anything we'd rather do than keep tasting each other!"

"Yum! I'd like some more, please!" Their laughter twinkled in the space that seemed to be between their bodies. "That is, if you're willing..."

"Oh, Jimmy, you already know the answer to that!" Jenny exclaimed. "Whatever's next, I'm ready and eager!"

"I knew you would be." Jimmy was only half-joking. It did seem to be that life reflected his desires if they asked for more love to show up. And in the "joining" with Jenny, the desire to love filled everything. "Level up!"

"Are we taking the elevator again, Jimmy?"

"Well, we did push the button again, Jenny!"

"Stairs are no longer necessary, Now."

105 JJ'S THOUGHTS

"Only floss the ones you want to keep!"

Jimmy didn't really like going to the dentist. He presumed that no one really did. 'Must be hard to be a dentist,' he thought. 'No one is happy to see you unless they've got a real problem going.'

Jimmy always tried to be cheerful as he waited to go into an appointment, but his insincerity probably shone through his otherwise beaming smile. 'They always seem to find something that needs fixing,' he thought. That's why he didn't like going to see the doctor, either. There are too many thoughts about the body falling apart. It made it difficult to keep telling himself, 'I'll never grow old.' Jimmy knew that the health of his body was a reflection of what he allowed the mind to regurgitate - if he could "Think and Grow Rich," like the book by Napoleon Hill, then he could. "think and grow old," too. The famous line of the book enthralled him: "Anything the mind can conceive and believe, it can achieve." This seemed to be true. And Jimmy was sure that it could work to the negative side of things, too.

He watched his thinking, brushed aside thoughts that were not "truly helpful," and tried not to lean into the future too much so he could stay in the "Now," but he still seemed to be growing older. His body seemed to be, anyway. If "He" had anything to do with the voice of the observer in his head, then "He" hadn't changed much over the years.

Jimmy had read a lot of books. His mind seemed to want more and more fodder until it didn't. One day, Jimmy had decided that "enough is enough" - that the truth that all the books pointed towards was the same, and instead of reading about it, he needed to implement the ideas - he needed to "live" the truth! Besides, he didn't like flossing.

Jimmy didn't like Brussels sprouts, either, but he didn't want to try to start "undoing the mind" with a thought so ingrained that he might give up before he shifted any thinking. He decided to start with "sleep."

"Sleep" was another thought that had deep grooves in the paths of his mind, but it also was innocuous in that it didn't seem to have a "direct effect" on the body. Jimmy had heard plenty of ideas about how much sleep the body needed, or even that it was the mind that required the resting phase, but in his experience, at least since he had been working construction, the hours that one slept could be minimized. The body could still survive and thrive. He had once believed that waking up before 6 a.m. was a grievous thing, but the pattern of waking at 4:44 for so many mornings to get to work by six had proven to him that he could change his mind about deeply held beliefs. Combine that with other "bodily needs" that kept him up late at night, and Jimmy's new mantra: "I only need 4 to 5 hours of sleep" seemed not only appropriate but inherently "true."

Jimmy began drinking less alcohol. There was an equation at work in his subconsciousness that said, "The more you drink, the more you'll need to 'sleep it off.'" Jimmy knew that conflicting thoughts only caused the mind stress, so he picked through his awareness for "matching thoughts" - those that he could align with his new intention. There were plenty to be found and many to be manifested.

Jimmy followed the prompting that was prevalent (and that seemed to work) that the Universe was not only "on his side" but had his "best interests in mind." Combined with the idea that the world was a reflection of his beliefs and thoughts about it, it was a simple progression to ideate that whatever showed up in his life was meant to be there, maybe as a clue to his next "move," maybe as an affirmation that he was "on the right track" in his thinking.

When someone mentioned the "Atkins Diet," he immediately seized upon the idea and bought the book. Jimmy's mind liked the idea that to respect his body, he needed to give it the "right food;" the world had taken him and many billions down the path of refined sugars and flours and chemical additives that were meant to preserve the food, not the body. Besides, he liked to eat meat and bacon, in particular! It was as if he had imagined this diet himself! Even peanut butter was a recommended food!

Jimmy adopted and adapted. He noticed that there were many other great side effects to this "new diet" of thought. He really did need to sleep less to feel refreshed! He began eating less, naturally. Or so he told himself. At first, his bathroom habits became "irregular," but that smoothed out in time. Maybe it was because he read that he would have more energy, or maybe because it was true that "you are what you eat," Jimmy noticed that he felt more creative and started writing again. He felt better about himself as he lost weight, slept less, wrote more, did more in the extra time that he now had, and looked forward to each new day a little bit more.

The "Atkins Diet" came and went. Jimmy's body weight came and went and came again as he allowed his mind to slip back into old patterns of thinking. He even started drinking again.

And then, Jenny.

Although he originally considered a relationship with her a "proximity infatuation," Jimmy found his mind wandering into the dangerous thought areas surrounding the concept of "Love."

Jimmy's body had once been his "temple," though he had given up on ideas of religion long ago. Somehow, as he opened his temple doors to allow this new congregation, the act brought with it ideas that he had also read about in books and attempted to live out in the apparent reality of the world.

At first, it had been an easy matter to push the "thoughts of love" aside. But the Universe kept putting movies like "Serendipity" and "City of Angels" in front of him, and, although he had seen them all before and felt them as surely as he might have lived them, the nagging idea of "true love" arose again and again. Even as he pushed Jenny and the idea of love away, it grew under his fingernails. It crept into spaces in his heart that had remained protected from the ravages of that love that had capriciously destroyed that very concept through previous failed relationships and lost dreams. And he thought about it a lot.

"Jenny, you know I'm different than other guys." Jimmy knew he was making last-ditch efforts to save his soul. "I'm not even the guy you think I am."

"Jimmy, I don't care if this doesn't last; I just want to enjoy it while I have the chance."

'Damn,' Jimmy thought, 'Why does she keep aligning with my thinking?'

"Me, too, Jenny. I'm just saying, I'm different."

"I like different, Jimmy. I've never experienced life the way I do with you."

Jimmy swallowed. "Just don't expect me to fall in love with you. That could be just a little too messy."

"The best things in life are a little messy, Jimmy. Like pizza or popcorn."

Jimmy loved pizza and popcorn! He absent-mindedly licked the index finger on his right hand.

"I know, Jimmy. 'If you lick it, it's yours!'"

Jimmy looked at his finger and burst out laughing. He knew he was falling fast for this woman, and soon, there would be no turning back.

"I'm licked, Jenny," he said, and they laughed until they cried.

"You are
what you think about
all day long."

14

106 JJ'S SWIM

"Why can't I say what I feel?"

Jimmy had lived enough life to know that it wasn't always "coming up roses." Looking around, he saw memories of every past time he had lived - the ups and downs, love lost, love found, people he had known, and those who had gone - all this now colored his mind. What more could he expect to find?

Jenny had shown up just like every other person he had met in the ocean of awareness - an interesting face, a somewhat new arrangement of stories - more context in a life that flowed from here to there, purposefully, it seemed, downstream in the dream.

He thought that he had seen her before, maybe circling the edges of his same group of friends, laughing at the same jokes and cheering the next story told over a beer and pizza. Like a shiny penny in the change in his pocket, she kept catching his eye, and he looked closer at the date and the engravings to check the condition. She seemed unique enough that he didn't let go, as there might be hidden value there.

And then they danced.

Jimmy had learned to notice what life brought to the shores of his ocean. He could always recognize an anomaly in the tides, his attention caught by the disruption in the otherwise catatonic flow.

Jenny had arrived with the music of the moment - a party of friends celebrating life by drowning the sorrow of it in the shared

15

song.

On a prompting, he had asked her to dance, to stand close for a moment, to share the rhythm of the story and the rhyme of the time. And he had asked her if he could lead the dance, and she had looked up at him and acquiesced, though the light reflected there told him that she followed her own promptings, guided by her own angels.

The moment had been exquisite and eternal, a reflection of the art of life, a partially drawn masterpiece provocative enough already to capture the artist's heart and pull him under to drown in a sea of his own creative intention.

Now, Jenny lived beside him. They dangled their feet from the shared dock and watched the reflections in the water dance, the ripples crossing one another again and again. They turned towards one another and smiled all the while, acknowledging the dream and knowing, beyond a doubt, that the day had been made for them to play.

"Jenny." Jimmy turned towards her form, though he could just as easily have kept his eyes closed and imagined her response. "Jenny, I..." He often lost track of his thoughts when her eyes met his. "Jenny, I think... we... should go shopping today." Jimmy wasn't even sure that was what he had meant to say, but here he was, years later, still tongue-tied by the beauty he saw before him. Luckily, Jenny had a mind of her own and knew, much the same as him, that love was meant to be spoken, like the magical language of elves or nymphs, whose lilt carried the song of life through unknown forests and seas.

"That sounds like a good idea, Jimmy. I think there may be things on our list that we could use." Jenny knew what she had said was a bit obvious, but every word that traveled the imaginary space between her and Jimmy served as a rope to keep their ships in sync. She also knew that the words didn't matter so much as the intent behind them.

"You're right again, Jenny! It's like the first time you said, 'Yes,' when I asked you to dance."

"I can't remember who asked whom, but I do remember the dance, Jimmy." She grinned with the light of the joy of that time. "And, sometimes, I think that dance has never ended."

Jimmy grinned, too. "Of course, it hasn't ended. And it doesn't

look like it ever will. The music hasn't stopped!"
    "I hear you, Jimmy."
    "I see you, Jenny."

> *"The ocean brings a wave from the deep sea*
> *and tosses it on the shore to wash the debris,*
> *to allow footsteps to make new prints*
> *on the sand of time."*

107 JJ'S TRUTH

"What we hold in the mind,
we hold in our lives."

Jimmy didn't like to think that things could go wrong. He believed or wanted to, that the universe always had his best interest "in Mind," so whatever happened HAD to be for the highest good. But it didn't always seem that way.

The furnace had been "acting up" for several years, and technicians had been there twice. It still short-cycled when it got really cold.

The internet sometimes "froze up," typically right in the exciting part of a movie.

And he didn't always find a "close" parking spot.

He had to admit that these were rather small things compared to the overall happiness that was so prevalent in his life now.

Now that Jenny was a part of it.

Although it seemed like life still played tricks on him - forgetting to put a cup under the Keurig, tripping the GFI that he couldn't find, "losing" his credit card in the other pants - recovery from upset was much quicker now. The joy of Jenny lifted everything up a level, more than twice as fun as life had been alone. This shared experience was many levels above what had been "the norm." So, Jimmy's mind recovered quickly from any form of "defeat." There were better things to think about, like whatever he and Jenny might do next, even if it was taking a nap watching Castle.

"Jenny." Jimmy's eyes fluttered open, and he slowly realized that they had fallen asleep, all snuggled up again.

"Wah, Jimmy?" Jenny hadn't quite gotten to the "eyes open" stage.

"I think we slept through two episodes..."

Jenny raised her head and looked at the TV screen. "I don't recognize this show."

"Me, either." Jimmy paused it with the remote. "What's the last thing you remember?"

Jenny sighed. "You, Jimmy. The last thing I remember is snuggling up to your warm body."

Jimmy laughed. "That's the same for me. I remember thinking that you needed warming up."

"I did, Jimmy. I do. Let's go someplace warm."

"Let's sleep on it a bit first."

"In in!"

"Remember, Jenny, if you say a thing again and again, it just might come true..." Jimmy's voice drifted off.

Jenny yawned and turned. "That's fine with me!"

"I love you, Jenny. That's true already!"

"Ditto, Jimmy. It's the best it's ever been."

"I like the way you think."

They laughed and fell asleep in each other's arms.

"Whatsoever things are true...
think on these things."

108 JJ'S OCCUPATION

"If the shoe fits...
you can walk a lot farther."

Jimmy was good at his job. He always described "managing" as "getting the right stuff there at the right time with the right number of people with the right skills to get the job done right."

And he was right.

The rest of his job requires imagination - taking the outline of a plan and putting all the right intentions in place to make it a reality.

These two ideas converged and, through time (and considerable effort), resulted in creation - something that wasn't there was now there, and it had a purpose in the world. When Jimmy looked at it, he could see the comparison to life in general. Maybe everything was a metaphor for something else.

Jimmy looked out the window at the snow-covered ground and sighed. He knew it was going to get warm again this week, and all that snow would be gone. Then, there would be things to do to help spring settle in: raking the yard again, cutting back the dead in the garden to make room for new life, and getting the patio furniture out again!

There was joy associated with these tasks, too. Knowing that one's efforts aligned with nature's and the natural order of things brought a certain satisfaction. He was a steward of time and space. Jenny worked side by side with him to encourage bright, joyful future moments.

"Jenny." Jimmy had learned from his Mother that it was more polite to always use proper names and not pronouns, like "hey you." "Jenny, it's almost time to break out the rakes and trim the garden!"

"Yippee, Jimmy! I can hardly wait to get my hands dirty!"

"Well, I'd wear gloves if I were you," Jimmy joked.

"But you ARE me!"

"Gloves, it is, then!" They laughed. "And I think we'll need one of those tandem bicycles so you can't ride faster than me, too."

"So long as I get to ride in front, Jimmy!"

"I wouldn't have it any other way. I can still be a 'backseat driver,' you know."

"You just want to watch my butt."

"Well, yes, there is that, Jenny."

"And we can golf again soon."

"We might be a bit rusty. When did we play last? September?"

"Six months on, six months off. We've got to move someplace warmer, Jimmy."

"I'm in for that, Jenny! Maybe your toes won't be so cold in bed!"

"You'll be glad that I'll wear less clothes, too, won't you, Jimmy?"

Jimmy whistled. "You know that's true!"

Jenny laughed. "I didn't know you could whistle!"

"That's one of the very few things you don't know about me. What will you do when I run out of stories?"

"We'll make new ones!"

"That's for sure, Jenny!"

"I can barely wait for spring!"

"Let's go rake the snow!"

"OK. I can wait a few more days..."

"Me, too. But we could take a walk and watch the snow melt!"

"That actually sounds exciting, Jimmy!"

"It's a plan, then! We'll try out our new tennis shoes!"

"You know it! I'm in!"

*"Everything is better,
shared."*

109 JJ'S QUILT

"The voice that calls to us
without speaking
is our own."

Jimmy knew the science, but he also knew that science comes "after," trying to explain a "why" or a "how" that may never have existed.

'Maybe everything just arises on its own,' he thought. And the more he thought, the more he felt that this was true; no explanation would ever do; the sky was blue because...

'If I tried to explain how Jenny and I came to love each other, it would be a story.' Jimmy knew that much was true. He also knew that every time he looked at Jenny, tracing the line of her profile with his eyes, and when she turned, falling deep into her eyes, the story didn't matter; just the feeling counted, and it amounted to love. "There's something happening here..." - the Buffalo Springfield song that played that fateful night when they first kissed - echoed what he still thought - "What it is ain't exactly clear." The rest of that song didn't matter. They had only heard those two lines again and again.

This script they followed might not have won an Oscar, but it became their favorite movie. And it just kept writing itself, and they rode the train of it, click-clacking in their ears, while they noted how smooth the ride really was and why they hadn't ridden trains more often. And the wind blew outside their windows.

"Jenny," Jimmy spoke her name into the silence as if it only took a whisper to bring her attention back to him. "Jenny, I was thinking, or 'not thinking,' really, that even though there's no 'real' control" - he emphasized 'real' - "I'm going to keep choosing this, like this, with you."

Jenny looked at him and smiled that bright acknowledgment that tickled Jimmy's heart. "Jimmy, this might all be a dream, but it's a good one. It's not the kind that you can't remember when you wake up. It keeps happening, and we keep saying, 'Yes, please,' and now being together is the best part of it!"

"Yes, please. Can I have some more?" They laughed together and then kissed quickly but certainly, acknowledging the point of focus that punctuated the story.

"I don't want to grow up, Jenny. I feel like I'm falling in love for the first time."

"It's like back in high school, Isn't it, Jimmy," Jenny spoke rhetorically, knowing there was no question that Jimmy felt the same as she did. "It feels so good, it's indescribable."

"That's it, exactly, Jenny!" Jimmy grinned excitedly. "It's like a miracle that is beyond explanation. Like we're skipping math class to go 'make out' under the bleachers because math doesn't apply anymore."

Jenny laughed. "I used to love math!" She looked at Jimmy, and her smile broadened. "But now only one thing adds up." And she leaned in to kiss him again, this time longer and softer than before.

"I guess we'll never quite know how this moment was woven into the fabric of our lives, but I sure do love the pattern!"

"It would be everyone's favorite quilt, Jimmy. And it would keep the whole world warm at night." They both laughed again.

"So long as we can pull it up under our chins, Jenny, I'm good."

They snuggled closer, imagining that there was no distance at all between them.

"Live in the mystery."

110 JJ'S EVOLUTION

"Wait a minute
- it'll change."

Nothing really stays the same. Life is sort of like time-lapse photography - a series of framed moments - that makes things that look the same reveal that they are moving.

The cells of the body change out constantly, some in a few years, some over a lifetime. Unfortunately, instead of living forever, the body becomes like a message faxed repeatedly - the imprinting gets a bit blurry over time.

The new couch gets a depression in it where we always sit.

Everything changes. Even the thoughts in our heads. Does all this evolution have a purpose? Or is it whimsical? It's a wonder.

"Jenny," Jimmy spoke her name as if it were the lyrics to a song. "Jenny, I keep wondering, not how we got here, but where everything is going?"

"Jimmy, you're thinking too much again." Jenny grinned, considering the philosophical flow that Jimmy continually revealed. 'Was it the Law of Attraction today,' she wondered, 'or something more existential.'

"Jenny, I know I'm not changing anything by thinking about it; life changes whether I think about it or not. But does the change really have some mysterious purpose about it, or is it merely random?"

'Existential angst,' Jenny concluded, but she said, "Does it really matter, Jimmy? Does our thinking have to have a purpose? Could perception just be a phenomenon to be experienced locally and presently without imposing a 'will' into the equation?"

"But how can 'I' not figure into it all? Even Nature seems to have a plan. And can't mankind destroy that plan by imposing his will?"

"Well, so far, Jimmy, the Mind seems to have noticed that some corrections could be in order, that 'sustainability' is a concept worth exploring."

"It looks that way, Jenny. It does. Maybe it doesn't even matter what I think about, so long as I act in alignment with my heart."

"Maybe that doesn't matter, either, Jimmy. Maybe we just live the best life we know how, given what we think we know and where we seem to be."

"That's probably the best thing to do, Jenny. Just 'Love and let love,' sort of!"

"I love you, Jimmy."

"I love you, too, Jenny."

"And, in the end,
the love you live
is equal to
the love you give."

111 JJ'S PROMPT

"Sex is what is different about us.
Love is what is the same."

Jenny and Jimmy had sex all day long. Jenny loved to play as a woman, and Jimmy loved to play as a man. Whenever they were together, they played the wonderful script that was written in the stars, two bodies dancing in space, circling one another, allowing gravity and mass and inertia to interact in the universal plot of "boy meets girl."

Although they had once rehearsed their parts, practice was no longer necessary. The play had become an everlasting improvisation, guided only by joy and wonder and the innocence available once they had dropped all pretense of "what it should look like." Love left no room for tension. Even foreplay (everything was foreplay) held no goal anticipation. "Making Love" really was in every moment. The physical act wasn't a culmination; it was another way that they expressed love for each other. They were so "into" love - "I'm All In" - that love colored everything they did, and they didn't stay within any lines, either. Jenny and Jimmy loved when they went to sleep together and loved when they woke up together.

Jenny grinned, looking at Jimmy. Each of their smiles shone a little, even in the dark, reflecting, perhaps, the light of each other's smiles. Like two Cheshire cats, they guided each other through the strangeness of the world, except that they also attended the tea parties together and never disappeared if they could help it.

"Jimmy!" Jenny always greeted Jimmy with a "welcome in" smile. "We did it!"

Jimmy always felt a rush when Jenny said his name as if the slightest recognition from this Goddess in his life made life worthwhile. "What'd we do, Jenny?"

"We made it through another night!"

Jimmy stacked his pillows up beside hers and slipped into bed. "Yes, we did!" And his grin definitely matched hers, even in the darkness. "I must be the luckiest man alive, waking up every day with a beautiful princess in his bed. Naked, even, to top it off!"

Jenny grinned even brighter (if that were possible). "Icing on the cake, Jimmy!" She wiggled her breasts a little to bring his attention there.

"Makes me want to lick the spoon, Jenny!" Jimmy pretended to swoop down on her chest like a seagull who spotted something on the dock it wanted to eat.

"What Goddess wouldn't want to wake up like this?" Jenny asked rhetorically to her "aside" - the imaginary guide that hovered above.

"Oh, my Goddess!" Jimmy laughed. "Me, too!"

They stopped to kiss like they did whenever prompted, and they were prompted a lot.

*"Follow the prompting
towards Love."*

112 JJ'S SLANG

"We're each unique.
And that's a gift to ourselves."

Jimmy never really did "blend." Looking back, he could see that none of his friends did, either. Now, he thought that everyone was "uniquely unique." Just like him. Only different.

In conversation, Jimmy still discussed whatever seemed to be "the daily news" - weather, sports, the economy - but he often steered the talk to something more than the "usual fare." Jimmy wanted to use his time to notice what's really important in life. Love. But it was sometimes awkward to steer a conversation to love in the midst of a bunch of guys. Or maybe he just thought it was, so it was.

"Jenny, I love you!" Jimmy said it often and in many different ways. He loved being with Jenny. She made everything a little brighter and more funner (er). More like Love!

"I love you, too, Jimmy!" Jenny had become drenched in the love they shared. They ate it for breakfast, lunch, and dinner. They danced it and romanced it, all because they chanced it!

"I'm so glad, Jenny, that we found each other in all of this world! I'm not a big believer in fate or 'god,' but if any Force in the universe had a hand in bringing us together, I salute it!" Jimmy saluted the ceiling and made a mock-serious face.

"Jimmy, we definitely fit well together! It's like everything else was just practice." And Jenny meant it. It didn't change how she loved her kids, but this life was so fresh and new and unexpected that she was "all in," no matter where it took them! Maybe even because it seemed to be taking both of them where they'd never been before. It changed how she loved life.

"Life is 'gooder' with you, Jen!" And Jimmy meant it with all his heart.

"Gooder is better than just good, Jimmy!" And she meant it, too!

"Love has its own language."

113 JJ'S SCIENCE

"Everything
has light around it."

An atom is mostly space, a proton circled by electrons that are relatively far apart. The electrons are pretty busy buzzing around in that "empty" space, though, dancing with some other electrons while repelling most. "Energy" - that invisible force that moves everything in the universe that we think we know - keeps these electrons in check so that coal doesn't become diamonds except under a whole lot of pressure. Alchemy became chemistry when magic gave way to knowledge. Does everything "stay itself" because we name it?

Jimmy always thought he knew a thing or two about how the world worked and his part in shaping it. And he had the pictures in his memory to "prove" it!

Influenced by all the books his elder siblings had left in their wake, Jimmy became a philosopher at an early age, espousing such principles as "First Thought" and "Present Moment Awareness." These belief systems served him well. Except they didn't. When Jimmy threw a wadded-up paper ball at the wastebasket, it didn't always go in, no matter the purity of his intention. And no matter (pun intended) how "present" he stayed, the past seemed to be buried in his bones, never to be released. Belief Systems, he very slowly realized, were imaginary frameworks projected onto a world that remained independently arising. Still, it seemed that his thinking could affect his actions in the immediate environment, although he

30

did keep banging into things that he hadn't anticipated. And he had learned that fresh ground coffee always tasted better. As Jimmy aged, he secretly wondered if the electrons in his body were slowing down on their own or if he just imagined himself growing "old," and that's the only reason that things didn't heal as quickly as they used to. Or was the turnover of cells in his body like the replacement of the people in his immediate world? Sometimes, the new cells looked just like the old cells. Sometimes they didn't. Nature didn't always replicate perfectly, but it did turn over its image a lot. Seasonally, even.

Jimmy did notice, as he grew "older," that even as he simplified his belief systems, titrating them and distilling them, the only prevalent "truth" that remained was that "things just happened." And "science" only happened after the fact. This did two things for Jimmy: it relieved him from the "need to know," and all of the impossible repercussions of "not knowing," and it developed a sense of indescribable joy that everything in life was a miracle and he wasn't responsible for any of it!

"Jenny." Jimmy always said her name as if he were trying to limit a miracle or speak to a Goddess. "Jenny, I think the same universe that brought us together is nudging us towards some new future. I can't tell exactly what it is, but it feels 'right' and good."

"I'm good as long as it nudges both of us, Jimmy!" Jenny was typically thrilled at Jimmy's awareness not only of what was happening "Now" but of what the future might hold. His prescience matched her intuition in a way that she had never experienced before, as if by focusing on the love between them, their very spirits became transparent to each other. "Hopefully, we're being nudged towards some warm place!"

"As you like it, Jenny! 'All the world's your stage,' you know!"

"Quoting Shakespeare, now, Jimmy?" Jenny's laughter sparkled in the space.

"Writing it, I think. Or rewriting it!" Jimmy laughed. "Some have greatness thrust upon them, you know."

"'To thine own self be true,' Jimmy!"

"'All that glitters is not gold,' Jenny! But we'll take it, anyway!"

"You do seem to be an alchemist, Jimmy."

"Things change on their own for the most part, I think, Jenny. We just get to go along for the ride."

"Shotgun!" Jenny said it quickly and loudly enough to startle Jimmy.

"I'm driving," said Jimmy. "And I'm SO glad you're along for the ride!"

"Me, too."

*"All experience
is imagination."*

114 JJ'S FIELD

"Seeing differently
is not being 'You' or 'Me.'
It's One, eternally."

Sometimes, when Jimmy thought about it, he knew he was
completely alone in his universe of perception. Yes, people had come
and gone, some showing up prevalently and some occasionally, his
own awareness the only constant. He had lived in different houses in
various places, and, again, he was the remaining witness.

Jimmy had never thought of himself as an existentialist - he barely
considered that he knew the term - often thinking that "It is what it
is" covered everything in perception. Later, he realized - made "real" -
the concept that "It is what we think it is" - and thus headed down
the path of Sartre and Camus.

Experience was, of course, comprised not only of his own
immediate experience, but also colored by everything he had been
"taught" (imprinted) as a child and later added to through
contemporary social adaptations. The idea of a "Morphogenetic
Field" intrigued Jimmy when he first read of it, making his own
contribution to "The Field" by changing the name to "Morphogenic,"
as, to him, it didn't have much to do with genes but more to do with
"fields of thought" and the resonance of these fields that allowed the
Mind to tap into universal information in a way that closely resembles
telepathy. "The Field" shared by all beings is localized to the extent
that the Perceiver "pays attention" to certain resonances while

ignoring others that are not part of his or her "wavelength." Jimmy's "Field," then, was most certainly his own. Thus, the other principles of existentialism - freedom and authenticity - were easily incorporated into the emerging philosophy that Jimmy utilized to "self-guide" his life experience. It was Jimmy's ultimate triumph to adapt Descartes' famous adage to: "I think Love, therefore I Am Love."

Jimmy sensed that the synchronicities that kept showing up in his life were somehow a product of his own developed perception of the relationship between the Universe and his mind. He often said, "The Universe is on my side," and he couldn't help but adopt the belief that this was true. The more that he anticipated and expected the miracles of synchronous events, the more he perceived them. The tendency to believe in his own psychic abilities was a direct result of this same noticing. 'Intuition is inherent in the Field,' Jimmy thought, 'and the circular reference is impossible to miss. I expect joy; therefore, I experience it and secure the loop in the Morphic Field for "others" to resonate with. As if there were "others."' He thought. 'How can I know anything other than my own perception of the world?'

And that brought him back to "It is what it is," his personal "Freedom" was that he was either responsible for all of it or none of it. Jimmy chose to love and let the rest of the equations wrestle with themselves.

"Jenny." Jimmy loved the way her name sounded on his tongue as if he could taste it, and the taste was that of Love Itself. "Jenny, do you think we'll ever know what brought us together?"

Jenny grinned. 'He's at it again,' she thought, 'trying to figure out why the world exists as it does.'

"Jimmy, I don't think that it's possible to 'know' such a thing. Life happens. For us, Love happened."

"That's the truth of it, isn't it, Jenny." Jimmy sighed. "I'm good knowing that you keep showing up in my life every day!"

"I hope that keeps happening, Jimmy. I'm counting on it."

"Well, so am I, Jenny! 'And wherever two or more are gathered in the dream...'" He let the sentence trail off, knowing that Jenny would finish it.

"There they are! I'm glad we dreamed of this love, Jimmy. It's a good one!"

"Ah, Jenny! If you could ever really know how much I love this dream of life with you, you'd know it had to be a dream!"

"People say we're dreamers, Jimmy."

"Well, we're not the only ones!"

"Sometimes, Jimmy, all I want to do is stay in 'JJ's World,' where 'everything is beautiful all the time!'"

"Is there any other world now, Jenny? We've 'gone all in' for Love, and that seems to have created a loop in Time and Space where we just keep waking up to Love every day!"

"And it's so yummy, Jimmy! You're all the things I ever looked for in a man."

"And you, Jenny, are the seeming compilation of every idea of Love I've ever had, too!"

"And so, it is."

"Amen."

"What we see
is what we get
all the time."

115 JJ'S INTUITION

"Present Moment Awareness - pauses the mind.
Just think - what you might find!"

Jimmy often found himself lost in thought. Or he lost himself there. With Jenny in his life, her presence interrupted his thoughts frequently. All he wanted to do was connect with her - a touch, a hug, a quick kiss - helped him to accomplish this. They chattered to each other, too, like squirrels in the same tree. Life seemed so happy and free now that the heart ruled and not the mind.

Amazingly, Jimmy noticed that his intuitive abilities had increased as he more frequently paused the mind, as if all of that thinking had clouded the energy field, blurring his connection to it. In Love, he was more in sync with everything and everyone, more likely to honor the aura than to analyze the action. Jimmy felt like hugging everyone! If he thought about it (and he still did, at times) he figured that his spirit had noticed when giving love, more love is returned. Hence, the prompting to Love!

"Jenny, have I told you lately?" Jimmy let the question hang there, as was their habit.

Jenny played her part with a sparkling tone and a whimsical smile. "I don't think so, Jimmy. And if you have, well, I don't mind hearing it again and again."

"I love you, Jenny." He laughed. She laughed. They acknowledged the obvious play of hearts and minds.

Jenny reached for Jimmy's hand and sighed heavily. "I suppose I'll just have to put up with it and love you back..."

"I suppose." Jimmy echoed with a sigh. "You know, Jenny..."

"What," she giggled.

"I never get tired of loving you. The opposite is true. I get energized by it!"

"Ah, Jimmy. I love it when you get all sappy."

"Evidently, I do, too!" And they laughed together again.

"That's why you're my 'Bestie,' Jimmy! Not to mention that you bring me coffee in the morning!"

"Two can enjoy life better than one, don't you think?"

"Everything is better, shared Jimmy. You know that!"

"Wouldn't that be a dream if everyone loved the way that we do?"

"I dream it more that way every day."

"Freeze, you owe me a Coke!"

"And that's no jinx!"

"A transparent heart
and an open mind,
all the wonders we'll find!"

116 JJ'S GARDEN

"Everything changes
It's all meant to engage us
Awareness a plus!"

Sometimes, Jimmy felt as if he was only now waking up to life. In this current flow of amazing love, he had finally realized that the dream wasn't separate from him, and was, instead, a symbiotic thing which both fed from him and he from it, sustained by the exchange.

Noticing how the movement of life tickled his perception facilitated his vision of a bright future. Light energy was bright energy. Coffee tasted brilliant because he imagined it so. The opportunity arose to move him because he had relented to the flow of the universe and lifted his feet from the sand to surf in the sea of form.

And Jenny.

When they had first danced in the whimsical universe of music and friends and laughter, it seemed as if the sun were peeking through a break in the clouds - the vision was attractive and demanded further consideration.

They each relented to the pull of an unknown future, seeing perhaps a glimmer of something greater together than they could realize separately. "And the joy they shared as 'they' tarried there..."

"Jenny." Jimmy felt excitement every time he used her name to connect. "Jenny, I was thinking..."

"Not again, Jimmy!" She laughed and poked his ribs.

"Yup. Again. Only this time, you were in it." He laughed with her. The dream of Jenny was prevalent in all his waking moments. "I was thinking that the universe wanted to bring us together."

"Because it did, Jimmy?"

"Yes, that. And because together we are capable of bringing more joy to the planet than if we were alone."

"We're the 'best we've ever been,' Jimmy!"

"Yes. Yes, we are." Jimmy laughed with her. "And it only gets better!"

"Do you think, Jimmy, that this is like part of the 'expanding universe' theory? That as things move and change, they are supposed to get better. Sort of like evolution."

"Well, Jenny, it's definitely part of the 'it is what it is' principle! And yet things do seem to get better."

"Maybe because we imagine them that way?" Jenny had a way of simplifying, perhaps distilling, to make things clear.

"Definitely that."

"None other... has ever... known."
~ C. Austin Miles (In the Garden)

117 JJ'S TIME

"Where the wind blows,
you'll find your soul."

Jimmy and Jenny seemed to know that life was meant to be lived as freely as possible. That is probably why the universe brought them together, although the arrangement took almost a lifetime to be discovered, or perhaps it was several lifetimes, either figuratively or literally. But now that "their time" had come, they seemed determined not to waste any of it.

Jimmy had always shared Ram Dass' "Be Here Now" spirituality, at least since he had read the book in "high" school. Even this philosophy, though, had a certain element of "Time" involved - some duality in a "non-dual" (perhaps) world. Could one know "Then" without "Now" or "Now" without "When"? Perhaps the Zen idea that the human perception is "faulty" would explain the "why." Jimmy had never been very good at meditation, either, and maybe the secret lay there somehow or some "when." Perhaps if he could quiet his mind completely, he would sense that he really was connected to everything in the Flow, and what he experienced personally was only an illusion of separation - that the ego really was just his personal story in the field.

Jenny had lived many lives, at least as many as she had children. As each child entered the world through her, life shifted. She had always known, somehow, that love had no limits, and the love she held for each of her newborns was the proof. Love only gets bigger,

40

she knew, or maybe it was "all-encompassing" to begin with, although that seemed an elusive idea in a world of "is there enough" or "how do we manage?" Jenny always felt "bigger" as each child was born, touching more lives as they did. And then, it was time for them to find their place in the world, and the split in perception was complete. Each had their own story now to tell. And she had her own to edit now that the context had shifted so dramatically. "Now," it was a choice, again, and a freedom that maybe she hadn't really felt before. "Now" was her time.

"Jimmy?" It seemed to Jenny that somehow he was always listening to her, that he kept a part of his awareness trained on her, caressing her with his love. "Yes, Girlfriend?"

Jenny grinned. Jimmy was not only her "boyfriend," as the saying went, but her "girlfriend" - sharing secrets, holding nothing back, laughing together at nothing and everything, friendship "thick with trust." She grinned, realizing this.

"Jimmy, I just wanted you to know that I really love all the things you do for me, but especially..." She let the sentence hang in the space as a tease to him.

"The way I tickle you? That I bring you coffee? Or is it the hot chocolate? I'll bet on the chocolate."

"It's the way you pay attention to me, Jimmy. I've never felt anything like that before. As if I'm never alone anymore."

"You're not, Jenny! I'm not only thinking about you most of the time, but I've tucked a little piece of me in your heart, like a GPS tracking device, so I can sense when it's time to go home and just 'be' together."

"That's it!" Jenny exclaimed. "You see? That's it, exactly! It's like you really are a part of me!"

"That's how we dreamed it, Girl! And our dreams have gotten pretty meshed now, so I can't tell where one ends and the other begins, and only by looking backward can I find any separation at all."

"Jimmy. Jimmy. Jimmy."

"Yes. Yes. Yes."

"I, I, I love you, Boy!"

"G... G... Girlfriend! I wouldn't dream it any other way! I'm SO glad that we found each other!"

"Me, too, Jimmy Choo. And that's a really tall order."
They both laughed.
"Jenny, you DO amuse me!"
"That's why I'm your 'Muse,' Jimmy."

"Go with the Flow.
Don't 'you' know."

118 JJ'S NOTICE

"You can feel the Zen
when you stop asking."

"The Mind is a terrible waste." Jimmy had made up this alteration of the UNCF campaign slogan - A Mind Is a Terrible Thing to Waste - to describe the existential viewpoint that he had developed reading "Non-duality" and "A Course in Miracles." The question "Who am I?" was certainly not answerable by thinking about it, writing about it, or reading Nietzsche. "I am not my thoughts" is probably the one thought that leads to the dismantling of the rest of the "thought system," as ACIM and Eckhart Tolle would testify. "The Peaceful Warrior" purports that "There's never 'nothing' going on. There are no ordinary moments." Jimmy had distilled his thoughts, feelings, and intuitions into the one phrase that, for him, summed it all up: "The Mind is a terrible waste."

No path in the thinking Mind led anywhere. Thoughts, like life, played out with or without his involvement. All of the labels that the Mind put on things to hold them in place were slipping off. Only Love seemed to remain shining brightly, like a lighthouse to a sinking ship. And thinking had nothing to do with it.

"Jenny." Of all the parts of the dream that he had lived so far, Jenny was the best. "Jenny, this is by far my favorite part of the dream."

"Jimmy, you know how to make a girl feel special! And I love you like there's no tomorrow!"

"Only Now, right, Girl?"

"Only right Now, Boy!"

"See what I mean? Quick mind, big heart. Hope we never have to part." Jimmy tapped her chest as he almost sang the last part.

Jenny tapped him back. "Big mind, soft heart. Can't stop loving once he starts!"

"I think you've gotten 'funnerer,' Jenny!"

"You've made me feel free to be me, Jimmy. And it feels 'gooderer!'"

"You're so right, Jenny! Feeling so loved lets us be free to express ourselves, doesn't it? That's a big, fat 'ditto' on that!"

"I prefer my 'dittos' to stay in shape."

They both laughed at that.

"Love frees the mind.
Only Love is real."

119 JJ'S SOURCE

*"Body moves in breaths.
Love's a sigh amidst the rest."*

At times, Jimmy was nearly overwhelmed by the amazing joy that love had brought into his life. He had been happy, but now life held new worth, art created by the broad brush strokes of rose-colored sight.

Even the night seemed somehow brighter. They shared the puzzles of life, not for the victory of completion, but for the time spent in joined perception, shared intention, and mingled invention. And with a little laughter, they moved on. Being "alone with his thoughts" was not something that Jimmy craved, though it seemed life gave plenty of opportunity for that "non-pursuit." When he paused, his mind turned to her like a shamrock turning towards the sun, leaves opening and flowers pointing toward the source of life.

"Jenny, I'll be glad when we can just stay in bed if we want. I just enjoy being with you." Jimmy had learned to say whatever was in his heart and on his mind, and the freedom of that always brought a smile with it.

Jenny smiled, too, and tilted her head at him. "That's funny, Jimmy, because I enjoy being with you!"

They were both grinning now, minds fascinated by the reflected sparkle of love in each other's eyes.

"We sure dreamed this well, together."

"Who knew that to have a dream life, all we had to do was dream?" Jenny laughed.

"That's what I love about you, Jenny! You're such a dreamer!"

"I dreamed you, didn't I?"

"I guess you did!" Jimmy exclaimed. "Our dreams have meshed somehow into one dream."

"That's how we dreamed it, Jimmy."

"You know me completely, don't you?"

"And I like every bit of it!"

"So do I, Jenny. So do I."

*"There are only
extraordinary moments."*

120 JJ'S GAME

"Alignment is what happens when no one's looking."

It certainly seemed to Jimmy that most of the time, the Universe worked; however, it worked, and he didn't really have much choice in the matter. But there were also times that it seemed that he had a choice to make - to be with Fate or jointly create.

"The Law of Attraction" seemed to be a great idea in the Mind - that energy had a vibration, and aligning with any form of it would bring it into awareness, and 'not aligning' could hold something back, like having the wrong contact lens prescription and not seeing everything that one was meant to see. But this argument was circular, begging on one hand that whatever happens - happens for a reason (vibration) and simultaneously inferring that one could change what one was experiencing by shifting perception (intentional resonance).

"The Universe Loves Movement." Jimmy had appeared to discover this axiom and assigned a meaning to it that "worked" with the rest of the seeming truth "out there." He had stood above stagnant ponds and noticed that life wasn't supported well there, and he had stood looking into the sparkle of a running stream and felt the gleam of new life, as if the glint of movement inspired life to arise, pulled towards a light from above.

'Is everything a metaphor?' Jimmy thought. 'Can a thing just "be" without some great revelation or spiritual vibration?' And the more Jimmy thought, the less he seemed to know. Every day, he awoke and was always glad of that. Every night, he fell asleep, dead to the world. When he awoke, it seemed as if the entire world rushed in, taking form again, "re-minding" Jimmy of how the world looked, even as it seemed to blur at the edges of his sensation. And he rode the wave of the arcing sun until the day was once again done.

"And it was good."

It always felt better to Jimmy to "own" the day, however it unfolded. "How do you know it was supposed to turn out that way? Because it did." This was his best guess, the simple Q&A that "fit" no matter what. Movement or no movement. Belief or not. Intention noted and included. Reason unnecessary, Now. "It Is What It Is" was a relevant subset. And the sun rolled around, and so did the next day.

"Jenny." Jimmy considered that Jenny had appeared in his life by some miracle of "Universal Grace," and he was a joyful recipient. "Jenny, I'm so glad that you're here sharing life with me. Your presence makes everything shinier!"

Jenny flashed a quick grin. "Ah, Jimmy! It's the best it's ever been, and we're the best we've ever been, ever since we said 'I'm in' to each other. It's like the Universe wanted us to be together."

"You're reading my mind again, Jenny."

"You dreamed me up that way, Jimmy, remember?"

"That's it, exactly, Jenny! I really believe that how we see life is a sort of waking dream. Everything is filtered by some wild mix of experience and best guesses in the present, but no one really knows what's going on. Just that, like a dream, it keeps unfolding. I don't want to wake up from this one, Jenny." He turned towards her and kissed her forehead. "I love this life with you, dream or not."

"Jimmy, you make me blush. And you make me feel like the luckiest woman alive! And it's always so fun! Who wouldn't want to wake up every morning with a smile and a kiss on the forehead? Oh, and a cup of coffee!"

"It's all a plot from the Universe, Jenny! I'm just following my promptings towards love."

"You do that well, James!" Jenny said formally, playing at being serious.

"Do I really have a choice, given my adopted philosophy of life?"

"Is it 'everything is love' this week, Jimmy? Or is it a variant of 'the Universe loves movement,' or both? 'The Universe loves a movement towards Love.' Hmm. I like that one!"

"And that's why I love you, Jenny!"

"Of course, it is..." Jenny let her voice trail off, inviting Jimmy to finish the thought.

"...that's how we dreamed it!"

"Love Is,
and All is well."

121 JJ'S PATTERNS

"Who is it that would take offense?"
~ Rumi

The greatest gift that Jenny had given to Jimmy was a certain realization that he was not alone. 'That's exactly what Love is,' Jimmy thought, 'It's giving acknowledgment to an "other" that not only do they exist, but that there is "good" there.'

Jimmy knew that acceptance was what we all were looking for in life. That's why Moms hold such a dear place in us - for their utter and complete acceptance of us when we didn't even know if we liked ourselves. And sometimes, Jimmy still didn't like himself. He still made mistakes, spilled things, broke things, said the wrong thing at the wrong time, tripped over his own feet, and didn't always brush his teeth before bed. He still held the idea that he was better than some others at some things, and that made him "special."

Jimmy's way tended to be the "right way" in his mind. Yet, in his deepest heart, Jimmy knew that this was all just a show, and what "he" did or didn't do made no difference in a universe that held everything.

Jenny made him feel loved. Love was the thing that made him want to live another day, to suffer the humiliation of all of his quirks and to laugh at them, releasing his idea of his "perfect self" and bringing freedom as he had never known before. And still, he occasionally pushed that away. Was he so addicted to his attention to himself that he couldn't give space for her to love others? 'Yikes!' Jimmy thought and didn't like the feel of it. At all.

"Jenny." Jimmy was so glad that there was a "Jenny" in his life that just saying her name gave him a thrill. "Jenny, I just want you to know that you're the best thing that ever happened to me."

"Recently, you mean Jimmy?" Jenny loved to tease him. It seemed that was part of her role in the relationship - to help him make fun of himself - which kept him humble and loving.

"Well, yes. Of course, other amazing moments have occurred in the past - a son, a great job, amazing adventures - but, yes, dammit, "recently" - in recent memory - YOU are the best thing that's happened in a very long time."

"I can say the same about you, Jimmy. And I do. And I thank you for being in my life, lighting it up with fun, joy, and laughter! You make everything fun!"

"Except when I don't. I know I can be a butthead sometimes."

"But you're MY Beavis, Darling. And that makes all the difference!" Jenny laughed and leaned her head back.

"I am kind of like a bad cartoon, eh? I can get so caught up in my ideas of how things should be done that I don't even see my mess on the floor."

"But at least you tend to stop and clean it up before too many other people have to step in it."

"Yup. I'm a great 'pooper scooper,' Jenny."

"You shovel well, Jimmy." They both burst out laughing and kept laughing until they had to wipe away the tears.

"Jenny, what will I do with you?"

"Just keep on loving me. And I'll keep on loving you. That's all we CAN do."

"And keep having fun doing it!"

"Laughter is the cure
for every possible offense."

122 JJ'S MOVE

*"Just a small shift and
changes begin happening.
Now will soon be Then."*

'Funny,' Jimmy thought, 'how things can seem to shift so quickly, and then you look back, and the idea was there all along.'

It wasn't that Jimmy didn't like things to change; it was just that he wasn't always as prepared as he wanted to be. Or as he thought he should be. Not that it mattered. He tended to always land on his feet, maybe like a cat - he did seem to have lived at least 5 or 6 different lives. He didn't think this was the "last one," but it certainly could be one of the best!

They had grown comfortable together, he and Jenny. The house really had become "home," where love is given and received and grows with time and attention. But there was more to experience together, obviously. There always was more, wherever it came from. And they were getting excited about it. They tended to be joyful every day, anyway. This move would be another context in which to play.

"Jenny." Jimmy turned to look at Jenny as he spoke as if the words hit their target better that way. "Jenny, I think we should give something to everyone."

"That's why we're having a 'going away' party, isn't it, Jimmy?"

"Yeah, I know, but I was thinking it would be fun to give them a plant or a book or a lamp or something. Maybe set up the garage with stuff and have each guest pick something out. They'll remember us for that."

Jenny caught the idea and got excited about it. "And we can lighten up at the same time!"

"Exactly! We have more stuff than we know what to do with, anyway."

"We can sort out three 'piles,' Jimmy. One for things we really want to take with us, one for things to have in the garage and sell anything left there, and one that needs to go to the Salvation Army."

"Maybe one more, Jenny. The pile of stuff to just throw away because we didn't need it anyway."

"Well, there might be an 'eBay pile,' too, Jimmy. For stuff like your Lego collection!"

"Pile it on, Girlfriend!" They laughed together.

"Sounds a bit like work, doesn't it, Jimmy."

"We'll feel so much better when we let go of more 'stuff,' Jenny."

"How does it accumulate so quickly, Jimmy?"

"A little at a time. And before you know it, you could be on 'Hoarders!'"

"I'd rather be on a travel show, Jimmy!"

"That's a 'big ten-four,' Jenny! Maybe when I retire, we'll become truck drivers and go cross-country!" Jimmy looked to Jenny again and, not seeing much excitement about the idea, continued in a quieter tone. "Or maybe not."

"We'll see when the time comes, Papa Bear."

"Changing channels, Mama Bear."

"Love isn't Love
till you give it away."
~ Oscar Hammerstein II

123 JJ'S JOY

"Laughing together
reminds us why we love."

Jimmy and Jenny both loved to laugh. If ever there was a universal truth, it could be that "laughter is the best medicine." Sharing laughter each morning was an amazing way to stoke the fires for the day ahead, and, followed by a longish hug, the Love Machine began chugging up the next hill.

On the weekends, they stayed in bed longer because they could, and the joy of just being together carried them into the dawn. They shared coffee in bed, exchanged stories and fluids, and generally affirmed that this - being naked to one another - was their favorite part of every day and was the best, if not the only, way to live and love well.

Nights played out much the same.

In the hours that they interacted with the outside world, each of them kept one eye on the clock and managed to "get things done" while keeping some heart and mind on each other. Love was the underlying theme. Love "reminded" them to judge less, forgive more, and recognize that the world flowed towards something greater than what appeared on the surface.

"Jenny." Jimmy's spirit lifted every time he turned his attention towards love, and Jenny's name represented exactly that. "Jenny, I was thinking..."

Jenny also turned her awareness towards love. This Love had turned life into a joyful place once again. It was the path "out of thinking" to a more feeling world. "Yes, Jimmy, you do tend to do that!" Jenny also loved that she could tease him and poke fun to wake that joyful bear that was more Baloo and rarely a growl.

"Ha! You got me there, Jenny! At least I KNOW that I think too much!" They chuckled and hugged a little closer. "But I really was thinking that the Universe does love movement, and maybe that's why we're always going somewhere and doing something."

"Jimmy, we've gone to more concerts and shows and movies than I have ever been to before. But the reason I love to go is because we're going together."

"'Everything's better shared,' you say, Jenny!"

"And you say, 'There's more where that came from,' Jimmy."

"We do dance well together, Jenny."

"Who'da thunk it!"

"That's the short and tall of it, isn't it, Girlfriend?"

"You know, we're the same height when we lie down. The difference is mostly in those legs of yours!"

"I like it when we go nose to nose!"

"Makes me curl my toes!"

"It's the differences
that make us the same."

124 JJ'S PLAY

"Love quenches every thirst."

Jimmy remembered (though more vaguely now) a time when Jenny wasn't in his life. Perhaps even then, he had dreamed of this easy conversation, the freedom of complete acceptance, and the thrill of amazing gratification. He just knew it hadn't always been like this, and now it was, and love suited him just fine. No explanations were needed. It was like coffee. Once, he hadn't liked coffee, then he had, and now he wanted it every morning. He rolled it around against his tongue and savored the flavors of it before swallowing and followed the warmth of it down, down, down... Jimmy lived for coffee now. And loved.

Life was never boring - there was always something to do, some new music to hear and dance to, whether to watch or walk in, somewhere to drive and talk on the way. When the dog had died, he had wanted someone to talk to, and had asked the Universe quite literally about it. He hadn't recognized that Jenny was the answer at first, but now... now that life was full of brilliant conversation, sometimes silent acknowledgment, and always bursting with love and laughter, he knew she had been the answer to that prayer. Now, he no longer needed prayers.

"Jenny." He rubbed the palm of her hand absentmindedly with his thumb while the thought unfolded into words. "Jenny, I sure do enjoy life a whole lot more with you in it."

Jenny looked Jimmy in the eyes and saw a reflection of her love there. "This, Jimmy, just this." She leaned to kiss his cheek, and Jimmy turned at the last instant to meet her mouth with his own. They kissed and broke apart laughing.

"You!" They each said it at the same time.

"Can we meet for lunch today?" Jimmy asked Jenny. His schedule was typically open and flexible, while Jenny's job sometimes called for lunch meetings with board members. Jenny kept a calendar on her phone that she used to remind her of just such meetings. She glanced at it, scrolled a bit, and then looked up into Jimmy's expectant gaze.

"It looks good right now!"

"It does, doesn't it!" Jimmy acknowledged gleefully. "But what will we eat?"

"We'll think of something, I'm sure, Boy."

"Yes, we will. And it'll be delicious! And tonight, we have that thing to go to."

"It's Friday night! The weekend seems longer when we do something on Friday night, doesn't it, Jimmy." It was a declaration, not a question.

"I'm up for that, Jenny! And for sleeping in tomorrow morning!"

"Let's hit the pause button and just stream this moment right now, Jimmy."

"Jenny, I am literally 'on hold.'" And he reached his arms around her, enveloping her with his attention, and it was good.

"Choosing 'happy' in the dream
brings everything into that focus."

125 JJ'S AGE

"Age is a state of mind."

"It's simple," Jimmy said, "Love gave us younger minds!"

It was true. This Love held nothing back, kept the mind from seeing lack, and never felt attacked. There was great freedom in that state, almost like having the mind of an imaginative child when the "consequence" of play is only joy.

"I get younger every minute," Jimmy said, "because you are in it!"

Jenny grinned with her playful friend. "I see you're entering puberty again."

"Except I've got more wind!" Jimmy explained, expanding on the concept. He took a deep breath and let it out. "See?"

"You're full of wind, all right," Jenny tossed back as if playing catch on a not-too-busy street.

Jimmy caught the ball and tossed it back.

"They call me 'The Breeze'. I keep blowing down the road."

"Sing it, Jimmy!"

"Ain't no change in the weather. Ain't no change in me."

"Well, except for the regression part."

"There is that," Jimmy responded, in his "normal" voice this time. "You'd better kiss me before I get too young and think it's 'icky,' Girlfriend."

Jenny laughed and kissed him passionately. "You'll never think that, Jimmy.!"

He pretended to stagger backward, losing his balance. "Dang, Girl, you should warn a guy!"

"That would take away part of the fun!" Jenny protested. "You

58

wouldn't want that."

"No. No. I wouldn't. I'm really getting used to all the fun again." And he kissed her back.

"Youth knows no consequence."

126 JJ'S SCENE

"In the big picture,
we're still just a lot of small pictures."

'It's an amazing, sustainable (almost) dream,' Jimmy thought. 'Much remains the same, yet all the while, things slowly change or rearrange until one day everything is different.' Jimmy sighed. 'Here I am, in the same house I was in 10 years ago (which was a big change, then), but it is entirely different when shared. Life with Jenny has completely replaced "life without Jenny," and I couldn't imagine it any other way now. This place that we share has become "our place." This world has become "JJ's World." This is our time. This is Love known differently a step at a time to the edge of the cliff and then... jumping and free falling.' Jimmy pictured himself falling through the darkness (the unknown) and through light (the good stuff). And even in his imagination, the falling became natural, with no fear of a "bottom." He grinned.

'Not sure what today will look like, but I know how it will feel.'

"Jenny." He turned towards her in the dark so his words could more easily reach her. "Jenny, are you awake?" He said it softly enough that she could ignore the call and loud enough to pierce the veil of sleep if she were near the end of it.

There was a pause. Jimmy let his mind and expectation coast.

"Mmmph. Jimmy. I'm wakie."

"Awesome! Are you ready for coffee?"

"I am, but I want a hug first." She slid over in the bed to align her body with his. "Is that OK?"

"More than OK, Jenny! It's all I really want in life!" He turned into her and kissed her forehead. "Maybe I don't want to get up to make coffee now." He teased her a little.

"Then I'm going back to sleep." Jenny tended to "win" teasing sessions unless he tickled her ribs until she went for her "safe word." This morning, Jenny didn't wait for the tickle.

"Hooty hoot." She called for an end to teasing and a beginning to caresses and softer expressions of love.

Jimmy took the cue and tucked some of her hair behind her ear. "You wake up looking so amazingly beautiful!"

"Lucky for me, it's still dark out. Now go get coffee."

"Yes, my love!"

"Everything I do, I do for you.
You are me.
Everything I do, I do for me."

127 JJ'S HOME

"They say you can't go home again,
but home is where you love, amen."

Jenny knew that life had never been this good before. She hadn't given anything up to get this love; the time had just been exactly right, and she went with the flow of it. Love like this was meant to be, had to be. The possibility hadn't been seen before. And now it was reality, however dreamlike it still seemed.

Jimmy knew that life had never been this good before. Maybe all the times he had thought that he had loved he had just been guessing at it. Now, he knew. Although the storyline was somehow familiar, the plot had changed completely, taking him to a place he knew he was meant to love and be loved well.

They both knew it felt like home.

"Jimmy," Jenny said his name softly, just loud enough to interrupt whatever reverie he was engrossed in. He always heard her, as if he kept a part of his attention on her at all times that he was awake. "Jimmy, I'll miss this house when we leave, but we'll be starting a new chapter in our life together, and that will be amazing."

"Ah, Jenny! Just being with you is amazing!" This was true, and Jimmy knew it. It didn't matter where they were. It always felt like dancing. "We're going to share a new place together. Like when we first fell into love."

"We're still falling, Jimmy. Only because there's no bottom to it, it feels like flying!"

"Magic carpet ride!"

"Well, you don't know... what we can find..." Jenny started singing the Steppenwolf song. Jimmy joined her.

"Why don't you come with me, little girl..."

They sang the last line together: "On a magic carpet ride."

And they burst into laughter.

*"Love is meant
to be laughed."*

128 JJ'S MAGIC

*"Living day by day
involves a lot of play."*

Jimmy liked the way they danced, like making love. Or maybe they made love the way they danced. Jimmy couldn't say that one was more true than the other. Love danced them like some great puppeteer. Bodies pulled together and apart, movements sometimes smooth and sometimes not. Love always hits the spot.

Jenny couldn't tell if there was a leader in this dance. They followed the music, and their bodies moved with it, sometimes as if the dance inspired the rhythm and not the other way around. Dancing was freeing. They danced in their world and sometimes wondered when others noticed them, as they could only see each other. They danced across the great expanse, holding hands to take no chance, bodies moving in romance; free expression wasn't chance; Muskrat Love advanced. The air was like water, hearts like otters, and every time she spun, he caught her. God, this was such fun!

"Jenny!" Jimmy spoke breathlessly. "Dancing with you is the best!"
Jenny grinned and shook her head in agreement. "Like I've never danced before, Boy!" And she meant it.
"Girlfriend! You have got the moves!" Jimmy had his arm around her shoulders and was tilting his head towards her to see the light sparkling in her eyes.
'I could look into these eyes forever,' he thought. 'The promise of love is illuminated in them.'

"Ah, Jenny! When you look at me like that..."

"I feel it, too, Jimmy. It's like an awakening or dreaming in color. I see love beaming from you, reflecting me, my love pouring out to meet yours in the space, time left behind."

"Exactly that, Girlfriend!"

"What are we going to do about it, Boyfriend?"

"Skip down the cobblestones?"

"Feeling groovy!" (~Simon and Garfunkel)

"And In the midst of the crowd dancing there, they were completely alone with each other."

129 JJ'S JOURNAL

*"Life's uncertainty is
what keeps it interesting."*

Jimmy always wanted to know. That's how his mind worked, now, and as far back as he could remember, how it always worked. Some things he seemed to know from birth, or his body knew: how to breathe, what to eat and when, and what hurt. Then, there were things that he learned as he lived: how to throw and catch, mow the lawn, use a rake, fish, cook, clean, and stage a scene. These thoughts create a timeline of "when" - "before he knew" how to do a thing, and "after he learned." Jimmy had a story of when he had learned how to ride a bike, and certainly what that bike looked like (the "red monster"), and had a story of his older brother pushing him and letting go so that he had to learn or possibly die trying. He had hung on right into the neighbor's bushes. He had learned "the hard way." Unfortunately, there had been many things that Jimmy had learned the hard way by choosing the "wrong way" first. The "wrong way" typically involved some sort of pain, like the neighbor's bushes. Jimmy had been lucky and hadn't broken any bones, though he had managed to break his heart a few times.

"Wisdom" was having "knowledge" and knowing how to apply it in a given situation. Jimmy could understand "rain" and "dry" and use "intention" to go inside to stay dry. "Intention" changed an idea into a purpose, an outcome, a desire to be manifested. Intention changed everything he learned and even how he learned. When he learned an "intention" to treat people fairly - to not apply knowledge painfully -

acting in accord with his intention - sharing wealth or information in a "non-harmful" way - it felt good, both to him and to the others in his sandbox. Using "intention," Jimmy developed a sense of personal morality, what was "good" and what was "bad," depending on outcomes. This became part of his idea of "who he was."

"Intuition" was what he developed from projecting what he thought he knew using "intention" and noticing if the outcomes matched his knowledge base. Because Jimmy kept expanding his knowledge base - reading, doing, and learning - his intuition became a highly developed tool of his mind. He could almost know a thing before it happened.

It must have happened over time - the change of mind that allowed the world to unfold without him knowing what it meant or did or if it hurt or not, without pushing his intention or agenda or interpretation on what was happening - just letting go of the "need to know ahead of time." Jimmy realized that time was part of the equation, certainly. The time "before" and "after" a thing happened. But "Time" was an elusive concept. When he tried to define it, it moved. He could distinguish "Now" from "Then," but he could not understand where "Now" was arising from. Because he couldn't pin this idea down, he had to give up knowing anything at all. And allow the world to arise on its own.

"Trust" allowed that whatever unfolded was for some "highest good" - good for the most people possible, anyway. The idea of "Gratitude" arose when he "believed" - to know without proof or facts - that something was "for his good." Somehow, this idea was twisted around punishment for doing "wrong," as his father had used that very phrase in his deep, dark past. But Jimmy learned to trust, anyway. And it served him by allowing him peace of mind. If he didn't have to know, and he didn't have to intend, then life was good just the way it was. But it hadn't always been so. Things had happened that didn't seem to be "in his best interest" at all.

As concepts became more difficult to discern - to know whether they were "right" or "wrong" - Jimmy developed a sense of spirituality. Ideas like "the best things in life are free," "less is more," or even "the future is Now" became true. The more that they couldn't be proven, the "truer" they were. "Love" was one such truth.

Jimmy had been baffled by "Love" his entire life. He "knew" he needed it or wanted to realize it, but not what it was or how to get it. The idea of "Love" arose on its own, that much was true, but how to define it, how to "own" the truth of it, how to say "I'm in Love" without sounding hollow because he didn't know what it was - eluded him.

Until it didn't.

Until Jenny.

Jimmy had lived and lost many times before, and the pain associated with the "loss of love" made him a bit leery of declaring it again. So how did he get into this completely impossible place of loving so much that he declared it to everyone and anyone who might listen?

Feelings, he supposed. Ideas that arose from mysterious origins for unknown purposes. Intuition multiplied by Miracles. "Knowing" surrendered to "being." There was no plausible explanation. It simply was.

"Jenny." Jimmy almost always paused when he said her name, relishing the taste on his tongue and in his heart. "Jenny, I love the story of 'Us' even if I don't know how it happened, really."

Jenny grinned and turned towards him. "Jimmy, there doesn't have to be a story, you know. 'It Is What It Is, and it feels just right."

"I DO have to keep 'reminding' myself that this can't be explained, so quit trying to put a story around it." He laughed, and Jenny joined him. "But it's a great story, anyway!"

"It's the best story I've ever read, Jimmy. And we're writing it together!"

"Now that's 'a-Muse-ing,' Jenny!" Jimmy had learned to let his thinking flow in the moment, aligning his words with his feelings without trying to control them - no analysis required. It, too, was a form of trust that "being in Love" seemed to encourage. "Freedom of expression" made Jimmy feel like a kid again.

"We 'a-Muse' each other, don't we, Jimmy!"

"Why do you keep me around, Jenny?" This was a question that they ping-ponged in the play of words that they shared.

"Because you amuse me." They both laughed.

"I know I keep you amused..." Jimmy started singing the Rod Stewart lyric in his best raspy voice.

Jenny joined in, as expected. "... but I feel I'm being used."

"Abused, more like," Jimmy interjected.

"But you didn't use your 'safe word,' Jimmy!"

"Hooty hoot!"

"OK, Gomer!"

*"Joy is what happens
when the inexplicable
collides with the miraculous."*

130 JJ'S REVERIE

"Life is a series of half-remembered choices."

'Perhaps I've lost my mind,' thought Jimmy. 'And I had only just found it.'

Jimmy's lesson of "learned consequences" was poking its head up again like an unwanted dandelion. The "Law of Attraction" sounded real again, and Jimmy knew that he was forgetting something that he had known about life. 'If I could only remember what it is.' Jimmy thought. He knew that he had gone from the soft face of a child to the hard countenance of an adult, only to finally understand that life should be looked at like the child - with soft eyes - there was nothing to be done and no one to do it. No matter how many people seemed to be in the room, there were really only his thoughts to watch.

'The Mind is a terrible waste.' Jimmy thought, 'And somehow, it is the only game going.'

Stories trailed behind Jimmy like unraveling bandages from a sleep-walking mummy. Parts of the dream seemed to be as old as Egypt, ideas that moved through time like juggernauts, knocking down the columns of the templed philosophies only to find that more and more had been built. Perhaps time didn't exist. Maybe there was no "cause and effect."

'Life could be as simple as the soft beating in the chest,' Jimmy thought. 'Light pulsing in darkness. My life is just a shooting star. Maybe someday I will know, but today is not that day.'

"Jenny." Jimmy loved that he was no longer alone with his

thoughts, that somehow Jenny shared them, even imagined them before he did, and laughed at all of the same jokes. "Jenny, I think that I'll never know what really makes life go."

"That makes two of us, Jimmy. It's a really good secret, isn't it?"

"Too good. Why can't we just see what's really going on?"

"Jimmy, what if nothing really is going on? Would you want to know that?"

"I'm not sure. Sometimes, I think that's exactly what's happening - nothing. Nothing at all. And then it seems like everything is happening all at once. And that feels unsettling, too."

"Didn't you tell me just yesterday, Jimmy, that life is what happens when we're making other plans?"

"Well, John Lennon said it first, although there may have been some early philosophers who agreed with him."

"Like you?" Jenny asked, grinning like the Cheshire cat.

"There you go, again, Jenny, pointing out the obvious."

"It's part of my job description."

"Wanted. Muse. Someone to talk to who also talks back."

"Can we discuss salary options?"

"When the time comes."

"You said time wasn't real, Jimmy."

"Did I say that out loud?"

"Don't worry. I was only half-listening."

"Which half?"

"The part where you say, 'This is it. Just This.'"

"Oh, yeah. That."

"It's all happening at the zoo.
I do believe it.
I do believe it's true."
~ Paul Simon

131 JJ'S LYRIC

"The need to 'touch'
drives so much."

Jimmy sat on the couch, wondering. In his mind, he saw a mirrored image of himself as if he were "looking from the outside in." The Moody Blues lyric crossed the span: "We decide which is right and which is an illusion?" 'Emphasis on what "is,"' Jimmy thought. 'Maybe even this is an illusion? This idea that "I" am "realizing" at this moment is really a projection, but of what?'

Jimmy had studied "A Course in Miracles" once upon a time, and some message there now reappeared: "It is not difficult to change a dream when once the dreamer has been recognized." The "separated mind" does not "see" that the dream and the Dreamer are One, believing instead that this world is being dreamed for him to realize. But by whom?

Often, just as Jimmy was waking, the last snatches of some dream seemed to slip away, as if they and the world they lived in were real instead of an illusion in a dream of sleep. Sometimes, there was a feeling of melancholy, as if there were a loss in his not remembering the dream. But then the body reasserted itself as the ruler of the current dream, demanding a walk to the bathroom and desiring coffee with its dreamed effects of energy and vitality. 'Which came first,' Jimmy wondered, 'the thought that made the body or the body from which thought arises? Could both be equally dreamed?'

"Jenny." Jimmy often was astounded that Jenny was such an integral part of his life now. This dream seemed so real with its sensuous reality and heartfelt expression. The Love that she represented was such a precious gift. Had he given this gift to himself when he vowed to be 'all in?' He knew that this question could never be answered, and he was good with that. "Jenny, I wonder what we'll choose to do today?"

"Jimmy, for now, I'm choosing this. Just this. Being close to you and sharing love and conversation."

"Me, too, Jenny. Just sometimes I wonder if we choose what shows up in the play of today or if we are blindly following some prompting to travel a winding path laid out before us by Fate or something like that."

"Maybe neither, Jimmy. Did you ever think that?"

"Probably. Although most of my thinking seems to fade away as if it wasn't real to begin with."

"That sounds like a circular argument. A dream within a dream."

"That's it, Jenny! That's what it feels like more and more - a dream within a dream. But who is doing the dreaming?"

"One of Us, Jimmy. We're the only ones in the room right now."

Jimmy stared at the ceiling of the bedroom as if there were an answer hidden in the shadows playing there, a movement created by light streaming through cracks in the blinds covering the window. Nothing came into focus. He turned towards Jenny.

"I do love Us, Jenny. Thank you for showing up and staying."

"Love is a great dream to stay in, Jimmy. Maybe it's the only good dream."

Jimmy fell back on another song lyric, as the mind often did: "Dream until the dream comes true." (~Aerosmith)

Jenny picked up the verse. "Sing for the laughter, and sing for the tears..."

"I prefer the laughter, Jenny!" Jimmy couldn't seem to help the grin spreading across his face. And he could see the same grin mirrored in Jenny. Still, it was a small, sadder part of him that echoed the next words: "Sing it with me if it's just for today..."

"Dream on, Jimmy. I'm not going anywhere."

Her words kept Jimmy from continuing the lines of the song and brought him back to the moment.

"Yes, Jenny. This is where I want to be. It feels like home."

*"Home is that place
where we learn to love
and give love in return."*

132 JJ'S ANTE

"In a world of dreams,
choose happy scenes."

Jimmy knew that happiness was not earned, or discovered, or some consequence of "doing good." Joy was not part of some equation involving service to mankind or even "being spiritual." Love taught him with laughter that "Choosing joy" was what he was after.

When Jimmy looked at Jenny, the sparkle of love in her eyes lit his own, and he knew that he'd found home.

Jenny loved this new life with Jimmy. Jimmy was freewheeling, fun, and different from any other man she had known. The freedom that he carried was infectious, and she found that it lifted her spirit just to be around him. If you could be addicted to Love, she was. Her "number one goal" (and his, it appeared) was to share time, relishing the soft exchange of loving energy, attention, and intention focused on each other.

When Jenny looked at Jimmy, the sparkle of love in his eyes lit her own, and she knew that she'd found home.

"Jenny." Jimmy loved talking with Jenny - she understood him, mostly, it seemed, and she loved him in spite of everything she knew. "Jenny, I can't wait to see what life brings next. So long as we're together, that is."

"Life together is my number one priority, too, Jimmy. I love 'being' with you."

"It always feels good when we're together, Jenny. It's like 'coming home' when we come home."

Jenny laughed. "That sums it up, Boyfriend!"

"It kind of does, doesn't it?" Jimmy laughed with her. "Simple equations are the best."

"Like 1+1=1?" Jenny knew Jimmy's philosophy of "Oneness." Like always, she tried to make him grin the way that he made her grin. It was a circular thing, bringing joy to herself by sharing it.

"That's exactly it, Jenny! But you knew that already. I knew that you knew because I can read my mind, and you are in it!"

"Keep thinking that way, Boy. I enjoy the echo."

"Are you saying that's a 'grand canyon' between my ears?"

"I am. But don't worry, there are donkey trails down to the bottom."

"Ha, Jenny! You are a hoot!"

"Are you saying I'm an owl?"

"Smarter than the average bear, Boo-Boo!"

"What's in your 'picka-nicka' basket?" Jenny asked, chuckling and trying to sound like the voice of Boo-Boo in the Yogi Bear cartoon.

"Goddess, I love you, Jenny! We really did grow up together in a different time and place."

"Maybe that's how we both dreamed it, Jimmy. That we would have lots of things in common, but enough differences to keep it interesting."

"You're way more than just 'interesting,' Girl. You're mesmerizing!"

"I'm so glad you noticed," Jenny said in a high, lilting voice.

"Couldn't help but notice, Pilgrim." Jimmy put on his best John Wayne, then dropped into his "regular voice."

"Really, Jenny, I don't know how it came to be, but this - this is 'home.'"

"Home is where our heart is."

"Gotta hand it to you, Jenny."

"I accept and raise you!"

"But I'm 'All in' already!"

"Me, too."

"Whenever doubt creeps in,
return to Love.
Love is always true."

133 JJ'S AWAKENING

"Following the dream,
it was a beautiful scene,
both sides of the meme."

Jimmy tended to wake up early, some long-standing habit from working construction for so many years, starting the day early to make the most of the light. Sometimes, it made for short nights. Waking from the dream state to "reality" often involved a quick transition from "out of the body" to "back in;" sometimes, he stubbed his toe on the corner post of the bed, which always moved him into consciousness quickly. Drinking a cup of coffee often helped with awakening, too. Finally, the shower seemed to transform any remaining doubt that a new day had begun, and he had better get dressed and get on with it.

On the weekends, it was great to wake up like always but to be able to choose to go back to bed, having no particular place to go. Every day was a little different. Sometimes, he woke up thinking of some long-past event or of what happened just yesterday. Other times, it seemed he was dreaming of what was to come - some new place that hadn't happened yet except in the dream. Jimmy thought that was where many of his déjà vu moments came from - walking through a place or time that he had previously dreamed. This led him to believe in many things, timelessness among them. He developed a habit of pausing when asked about some "future moment" - "Do you want to go to the City Bar?" Jimmy would sort of "look forward" in time to see if he had gone - that is, if an image arose of him sitting at the City Bar. "I don't see us there" might be a response, or "It looks like we went!" This behavior blended well with his central belief system that said simply, "Follow Your Promptings."

Another main tenet of belief involved first that "The Universe is on your side." Although this still maintained a position that there was a "You" and a "Universe," it really was sort of a "You-Niverse," as the second tenet - "Go with the Flow" also included the idea that experience consisted mostly of a mirror of projected images. "Going with the Flow," then, actually meant to follow the path that one had laid out, acting in accordance with one's best intentions for one's self. As if - contrary to many an adage - he did know what was good for himself, on some level of consciousness or awareness. How could he not?

So, whatever happened, happened, and if he aligned with the thought that every moment was perfect, he really couldn't get upset if he stubbed his toe or ran into just the person he had been thinking about. Jimmy tended to go through life with a grin on his face.

"Jenny?" Jimmy often said her name with a lift at the end that made it sound like a question when really it was an acknowledgement of the pleasure of her existence in his waking moments. "Jenny, I really love your face, you know."

"This face?" She responded, grinning, and added a soft southern accent. "Whatever for?"

Jimmy laughed. "I think it's the grin that always seems to be there!"

"That's just a reflection of your own, you know."

"That's probably why it feels so good! I'm caught in this amazing loop where you keep showing up to reflect me to me, and I'm completely amazed by it all."

"You dreamed me, Jimmy. Just this way."

"I'm a great dreamer, then, Jenny!"

"We both are."

"I knew you were going to say that!"

"Of course you did!"

"This happiness loop really is the best. I've never been so continuously joyful before."

"Maybe we didn't have the awareness to choose this before, Jimmy."

"The timing is fairly perfect, isn't it?"
"We wouldn't have it any other way."

"I wake to sleep and take my waking slow.
I feel my fate in what I cannot fear.
I learn by going where I have to go.
We think by feeling. What is there to know?
I hear my being dance from ear to ear.
I wake to sleep and take my waking slow."
~ Roethke, "The Waking"

134 JJ'S PRESENT

"'Presence' taps into
a secret place within
and allows us to make the best choices."

Jimmy didn't kid himself anymore. He was a philosophy "junkie." Or a recovering one. He had finally quit reading books about belief systems and was actually working on limiting his own 'limiting' beliefs. And it seemed to be working because things were working out better now than they had before. When Jimmy allowed that the universe might work better without his input, it really did seem to do just that - things worked out. For the best, it seemed. All on its own. And Jimmy was free to kick back and be in awe. He still had to put gas in the tank of his truck and get the oil changed once in a while, but he didn't need to speed to get anywhere - did those few minutes really matter? The prompting from the Universe was to "take it easy" - and that was maybe the hardest thing Jimmy had ever done. "Letting go of the reins" seemed self-defeating, and probably was, to the "self" that had all of these ideas that it wanted to manifest all over the place.

Somehow, things kept moving along. As the Steve Miller Band reminded him - Time kept on slipping into the future, and he was learning to fly with it.

"Jenny." Jimmy knew that Jenny showing up in his life had only happened because he had let go of searching for anyone or any certain thing. "Jenny, I do realize that this life that we share is what I wanted all along, and yet I had nothing to do with it showing up."

"Ah, Jimmy." Jenny loved it when Jimmy revealed his innermost thoughts and desires to her. That was part of the reason that this life seemed so magical! She had never met someone so "open" before. "Jimmy, you and I dream well together. We were meant to be sharing this time and space. How do I know? Because here we are."

"You're so right, Girlfriend! Here we are. 'Be Here Now.' What's weird is being able to 'see' our future together and knowing that 'staying present' is the best way to get from here to there. Allowing life to unfold, I guess."

"I think we're better off not thinking about it, Jimmy." They both laughed.

"So long as there are hugs involved!"

"Spooning or 'full frontal,' Boyfriend?"

"Yes."

"Life's simple pleasures
are full of Love."

135 JJ'S LAUGHTER

"Everything is better... shared."

Jimmy knew that he liked sharing life with someone a lot more than he liked being alone. Looking back, he could really see that's why he went out to bars and bands, looking for someone who would dance with him, looking for a friend who heard the music the same way that he did, looking for a lover who cherished touch the way he yearned for it. But it wasn't until he quit looking that she showed up.

Maybe he had been trying too hard, projecting his ideals onto anyone who showed up, only to be disappointed when they didn't live up to the dream.

So, he quit dreaming.

And then, Jenny.

"Jenny!" Something inside Jimmy always lifted his spirit a little when he said her name as if it held all the magic of her that had dazzled him so completely. "Jenny, do you know that we've been living together for almost three years now?"

"Time flies when you're having fun, Jimmy!" And Jenny knew that she had never had so much fun as she did with Jimmy. And it showed in her eyes.

"That's SO true, Jenny! It is SO fun sharing time with you! There are so many things I wouldn't have done without you being with me. Thank you for being with me." Jimmy's voice softened as he spoke those words, the Love behind them evident in the flow.

"Thank you, too, Jimmy." Jenny's voice reflected his, light with

36

love. "I love sharing life with you. Everything is 'funnerer,' you know."

"I know it's 'betterer' now than it ever has been before!"

They laughed together, as they liked to do. It had become a habit to laugh now that Love had become a constant.

"And freer...-er!"

"No truer-er words were ever-er spoken, my Dear-er!"

"Elementary-er, Doctor-er Watson!"

And they laughed because that's what they did together.

*"Laughter frees the heart and the mind,
so find someone who laughs in kind."*

136 JJ'S DREAM

*"I used to have to remember
to 'choose happy' in the dream.
Now, with you, the dream IS happy!"*

Jimmy used to wonder if this was all some fantastic daydream, and the more he read and lived, the less inclined he was to believe otherwise. And that proved to be a good thing.

In his dream of consciousness there was a spark of intention or spirit that seemed intrinsic to the dream and also the light of his life within it. Did it grow to become the Observer? If he traced the projection back to Source, to the projector, was this the cord that led to the plug that tapped its power from some greater Source? Or was this, too, a part of the dream? An impossible meme, for sure.

Allowing the idea of "free will" seemed the most fun - almost joyous in Time - so that was the way that he went. Maybe that was his only choice, this one voice that said, "A dream? I'm in!"

The idea of Jenny had always been there, at least as far back as memory could go. Every great writer throughout time had explored the idea of Love and, not managed to encapsulate the feel of it as it happened, had been unable to say, "This is it." Jimmy knew the feel of it and recognized the joy of it without understanding the origin of it. If there was one thing that he had learned in his many years in the dream, it was that he could know nothing for certain, including who and what he was and why "he" felt as he did. He learned to live with that. Matter was not a fact. Love was where it's at. In this moment of Now, the dream unfolded splendidly, and that was enough. There still seemed to be "things to do" and "things to get done," but nothing held his awareness like this idea of Jenny, these thoughts of Love, this feeling of Joy. The Boy had looked and looked for this as an adult and only found it when he had quit "Adulting" and "retro-verted" to the ways of youth. He was happy, and he knew it.

"Jenny." Her name now represented the joy of life, and Jimmy always grinned when he said it. "Jenny, have I told you lately...?" It was part of the meme in the dream that he would say this and that Jenny would answer, fluttering her eyelashes and flourishing a grin and a southern accent.

"Why, no, Jimmy. I don't believe you have, but even if you have, I never grow tired of hearing it."

Jimmy would sometimes blurt out, "I love you, Jenny." Other times, he would embellish, "I love you like the moon loves the sun, which gives it light for all the world to see." Either way, the light reflected in Jenny's eyes was definitely a match to his own, like the moon and the stars and Venus and Mars. The same, only different. One, as if Two. Who could argue the beauty of the view?

"I just love This, Jenny." Jimmy emphasized "This" and waved his arm in the air to include everything that he could see. "This amazing dream of you and me, here and now, with all of the pending adventures to be shared."

"I can hardly wait to get started, Boyfriend!" And she meant it. "This is all I ever dreamed love could be, and we're not done dreaming yet!"

"Exactly, Jenny! We've only just begun..." Jimmy sang the last, mimicking the Carpenters of his past dreams.

Jenny leaned in and kissed his cheek. "A kiss for luck, and we're on our way..."

Now, they sang together, and each could feel the flow of love and the future in the lyrics, in the flesh.

"Sharing horizons that are new to us. Watchin' the signs along the way."

Looking into each other's eyes, they could only see one thing.

"And when the evening comes, we smile. So much of life ahead..."

"And yes,
we've just begun..."

137 JJ'S PUZZLE

"We take our waking slow..."
~ Roethke

Jimmy wondered, at times, just how the body seemed to pull his awareness out of one world of dreams into another. As he awoke to this world that seemed to have more continuity, he often tried to drag the feeling of the other world with him. Or it stayed with him, stuck here and there in his mind, falling off him as he swung his legs, using the weight of them to pivot his body up and off the bed, standing to clear his head and find some balance, then walking to the door where life began anew.

'I like waking up here,' he thought. 'I hope it keeps on happening.'

Jimmy turned to look back at Jenny's sleeping form, listening closely to hear her light, steady breathing, knowing she dreamed but not what she was dreaming. 'I'm so glad she wakes up to this world with me every day. Life's always better when we're together.'

Jimmy turned and walked to the bathroom, noticing places where his body had healed a little in the night when his mind was focused elsewhere. 'I'm sure glad it's on autopilot,' he thought, as he splashed water on his face and rubbed his eyes, then looked in the mirror, all without turning on a light. The glow of the small night light plugged into the wall was enough. He wasn't ready to focus directly on this world. He preferred to take it slowly, awareness blinking his mind clear, the mirror reflecting darkly. If he looked too closely, too quickly, the magic was undone, and history snapped back into place, and he could no longer see the traces of light at the edges of night.

"Jenny." He said her name softly so it didn't pull her too soon from whatever dream she was tending. He wanted her to join his dream. His mind seemed to tug at hers to wake up to him. And she did, with a muffled yawn and a muddled noise that could have meant "Good morning."

"Good morning to you, my Dear One." Jimmy leaned over to kiss Jenny's cheek. "It's time."

"Time for what," she said, stretching again and turning towards him in the bed.

"Time to play, of course!" Jimmy loved how they shared this waking to the world, sharing glances and soft conversation until light crept in around the edges of the windows. "What else is there to do?"

Jenny pulled her body up to an almost sitting position next to Jimmy. "That's all I want to do," she said. "Is there coffee involved?"

"Why, yes, there is!" Jimmy exclaimed and reached for the second cup sitting on the nightstand beside him. "Here is your magical elixir," he said, handing it to her carefully, allowing her hands and mind to feel the solidity and the weight of it before letting go.

Jenny sipped it slowly, with her eyes closed. "I love the feeling of the warmth flowing down inside me. It's yummy."

Jimmy sipped his coffee, relishing the taste that surrounded it. "Mmm, Mmm, good." He mimicked the Campbell's soup jingle. "That's how Jimmy makes it..."

Jenny finished the jingle. "Mmm, Mmm, good."

"Just like life with you, Jenny!"

"A little salty?" Jenny quipped.

"That's it, exactly!"

They laughed and then began sharing the puzzle of the day, imagining words to fill the spaces, enjoying the playful clues, and turning to look at the amazing views.

"It's all up to you,
whatever you do."

138 JJ'S WAVE

*"Sometimes, when we look ahead,
we miss where we're at."*

Jenny was excited to join Jimmy on yet another adventure! They
had been looking at places to live and had finally been led to an ideal
locale. The excitement of moving had them looking far into the
future, where they sat on new patios under a different sun, discussing
air conditioning and camping - new fun!

But first, they had to slowly let go of the place and time that they
had called home for so long. They had begun by taking things down:
glasses, books, tax records, Christmas ornaments. And they ate their
way through the freezer and used up the "spare" this and that, from
paper towels to toothpaste. There were clothes to go through, tools
to sell, and boxes of stuff to give away. Too many TVs, surround
sound systems, and pictures were still on the walls - the collection
had grown with their relationship - and now included a "home
office," a sauna, and enough yoga mats to carpet the living room.

"Do we need a storage unit?" Jenny asked, looking and mentally
listing all the things that they wanted to take with them and counting
all the trips that they would take.

"Wow, Jenny! That might be just what we need, although I hate to
handle things twice."

"It's not efficient that way, is it?" Jenny grinned broadly. She
enjoyed poking fun at his "Jimmy-isms," and "economy of motion"
was one of them. He often tried to do too many things at once,
having too many balls in the air, until he dropped one and then

started over.

"Definitely not! But it could be essential to a successful operation!"

"Our 'home-ectomy?'" Jenny ventured coyly.

"Home is where the heart is, of course. That's everywhere that we are. But..." Jimmy took a deep breath, looked around, and let it out as a sigh. "We have some good memories here!"

"Yes, we do, Jimmy. But we'll take those memories with us. And make new ones!" Jenny's eyes gleamed with her vision of their future together.

"You're so right, Girlfriend!" He reached for her as if to hug, then tickled her ribs first before pulling her close. "All I really want is someone to talk to, anyway." Jimmy was referring to his story of how he asked the Universe (out loud) for just that. And then he had almost pushed away the answer to his prayer.

"She's right here in front of you!" Jenny poked fun at Jimmy's story of how he had heard a voice distinctly say those words right after he had spoken about "Love Right Now" at a family "celebration of life."

"And I'm 'All in,' Girlfriend!" Jimmy looked into her eyes, and she could see and feel the truth of that in his face.

"Yes, you are!" She confirmed, then added, "Me, too!"

They kissed and long-hugged, the kind that is meant to go on forever. Then Jimmy broke the embrace.

"Let's get this adventure packed up so we can start a new one!"

"I'm in!" Jenny exclaimed. They both looked around and said it almost simultaneously:

"We need more boxes."

"Goodbyes aren't hard when you take the love with you."

139 JJ'S SUN

*"Let's go somewhere new,
someplace with a warmer view."*

Jimmy knew winter. He had grown up liking snow and a little cold, except when riding his bike in it to deliver the local newspaper. His toes got so cold that he couldn't feel them sometimes, and they stung as they warmed back up, like the pain of healing. Besides learning that he liked money and could be persistent, he discovered that he didn't like the cold and its effects on the body. Even his fingers agreed.

Jimmy had been born in the winter, but he never was a skier or much of an ice skater, either. He enjoyed sledding in his youth, although the walk back up the hill wasn't much fun, and he and his siblings found that plastic sleds work as well, traveling down a grassy hill as a white one.

When Jimmy moved out west, he discovered a different kind of winter - colder and biting. Yet the folks who lived there had learned to embrace the cold face and icy breath of the place. But Jimmy was glad that life took him gradually south, and the winters grew milder and warmer until the sight of snow became a rarity. He didn't miss it.

Life had taken a turn, though, and sent him back north, where the seasons were dramatic, and love was a bit tragic. And Jimmy had learned the phrase "It Is What It Is." Long winters did that. And they made the sweet warmth of summer a special time that called for as much camping and outdoor activity as possible.

Jimmy's mind often turned towards sunnier times, when the hot sun had baked him and the earth, and he took trips there to remember, and life arranged for longer stays where he could enjoy the escape from the jaws of winter.

Now, he would return to that warmth. And life had given him the best partner to make the trip! Jenny had been born in spring and had survived less winters than he had, but she was ready to get hot again!

"Jenny." Jimmy always warmed in his heart when he turned his attention towards this amazing woman. He could feel it in his voice. He knew she felt it, too. "Jenny, I can't wait to go south again!"

"Me too, Jimmy. You know how I like to stay warm."

"You'll be warm to your bones and hot to the touch!" Jimmy laughed, feigning burnt fingers as he touched her arm and then pulled it away.

"And we'll both be able to tan our legs again!" Jenny exclaimed, holding a white leg up and then pulling the covers over it again. "But most of all, you won't have to warm me up all the time!"

"It's SO exhausting, you know, Jenny." Jimmy played his part dramatically, making a face to match the drawn-out voice. "I don't know what I'll do with all the extra time!"

"We'll think of something," Jenny offered with a wink and a grin.

"Hopefully, it will involve staying warm, Girlfriend."

"You know that it will, Boy."

"Sizzling scenarios, Batgirl!"

"Riddle me this, Robin. What has four legs, two heads, and is too hot to handle?"

Jimmy pretended to think a while, then blurted out the obvious answer: "Us!"

"Life is a game to be played.
You get to make up the rules along the way,
but you can't get off the board
until your ticket is punched."

140 JJ'S BIKES

"Can you imagine life so fine,
that you're grinning all the time."

Jimmy laughed too loud. At least people sometimes told him that. He shook it off with a literal grin, knowing that to laugh is a win, and loudly was no sin. It seemed to him that everyone could use a laugh that shook their bones and said, "You're not alone." Jimmy knew that joy had found a home in him, and he was keeping it by exercising it and taking it along for the ride. When Jimmy was happy, it seemed that everyone around him was happy, as if mirroring him. 'Maybe that's exactly how it works,' he thought. 'Life is a reflection of me.' He grinned at that idea and knew that it was likely true.

Jimmy used to wonder what everyone else was thinking. He had thought quite a lot about things - what made them work, what made them happy, how everyone looked at life - and wondered if he was the only one who thought about things the way that he did, or was he alone in that, and on his own in life. But he had been afraid to say what he was thinking in case he was wrong, and they laughed at him. Later in life, when he had grown strong in his own beliefs, he shared them freely and laughed at everything that he had once believed and even what he now believed, knowing that, mostly, life really did mirror what he was thinking and feeling. The game was so much more fun this way. Life kept rising, and Jimmy kept playing like a slow game of "whack-a-mole."

And then, Jenny.

Jenny increased the intensity of the game. In this crazy love, there was immediate reflection and instant gratification and a mathematical progression of joyful communication that rivaled life's perfection!

"Jimmy!" Jenny enjoyed interrupting the reverie that Jimmy sometimes fell into. "Jimmy, what are you thinking about?"

"Nothing much, girly girl. Just how fun the world is with you in it."

"You say the sweetest things," Jenny said coyly, employing her Southern charm. "You could sweep a girl off her feet!"

"That's the idea!" Jimmy laughed and reached to tickle her ribs. "And you'll be laughing all the way!"

"I'm counting on it," Jenny responded as she pretended to elude his tickling fingers. "It was your joyful disposition that attracted me primarily."

"That's a big ditto on that, Girlfriend." And he broke out into a slightly mangled lyric of Rod Stewart's Maggie May: "You laughed at all of my jokes, my love, you didn't need to coax."

"You are a fun guy!"

"There you go, calling me a mushroom again."

They were both sure that they had never been quite so happy before, and they were just as certain that their future together would be more of the same.

It was their world, and they were happy to keep it that way.

"Life is a reflection,
emanating from the Perceiver
in a close cycle."

141 JJ'S BIRDS

*"Can you hear the past,
like the sound of trains in the night,
echoing in the dark?"*

Jimmy knew "What's past is past, leave it where it belongs" was a great way to live, free from previous beliefs held about the world. He also knew that who he was today was partially a painting made of all the brush strokes of every moment he had seemingly lived. Jimmy believed that the future was pulling him forward into new experiences every day, as it played with energy and light, day and night, and all the colors of our sight. It was as if he lived only as a focused moment in time, and the feeling of that was so sublime.

The presence of Jenny in that focus had become natural and visceral, as if this love had always lived in his very bones, calling him home like the trains of his childhood, their deep call echoing across his mind as they pulled into town.

Everywhere he looked, life was good. The perfection of it shone in the faces of those who rose in the dream, who danced and played, worked and strained, and celebrated the world that they'd made.

And Now, Jenny.

Jimmy had loved before. The feel of it was no stranger, having broken the heart of him repeatedly through the years. But this love seemed to supersede the rest, built on the ruins of the lost cities of hope and prayer. Now, neither of those held a place in his mind - this love just "was" - no explanation needed or even possible. He woke to it, spent every moment in it, and fell asleep dreaming in it. It was the blood of his life.

"Jenny." In Jimmy's mind, Jenny was ever-present, as if he called his name to bring a feeling into focus. 'Jenny, can you hear the birds singing this morning?' Jimmy thought it as he sat in the dark of another room in the house, directing attention towards the form of love resting quietly and still in bed as if he could project the idea down the hall and into her dreams.

"Jenny, do you mind if I wrap myself around you?"
"It's my favorite position, Jimmy."
"Mine too. There's nothing I'd rather do. Until my arm falls asleep, that is!" Jimmy laughed and moved his arm, shaking it as if to wake it up. "For an imaginary arm, it sure tickles sometimes!"
"Imagine that, Jimmy!" Jenny said and turned over onto her back. "I've got an imaginary hip like that!"
"I want to 'see things differently,' Jenny. Got any ibuprofen over there?"
"These aren't the psychedelic ones," Jenny joked, handing him the bottle from the drawer of her nightstand.
"Darn! I guess 'pain-free' will have to do."
"Want me to kiss it and make it better?"
"Well, I'm not sure that would work, but we could give it a try!" Jimmy loved Jenny's playfulness, likewise for Jenny.
"Everything is fun, isn't it, Boyfriend!"
"With you, it is, Girl. Or maybe we're just making it all up, and we've figured out that there really is nothing to worry about."
"I'll go with that, Jimmy." She hummed the lyric to Strawberry Fields: "... nothing to get hung about..."
"It all works out, doesn't it."
"We wouldn't have it any other way."
"Let me take you down..."

"Dream until the dream's untrue."

142 JJ'S CROWD

"Seeming shared perception
always leads the right direction."

Jimmy passed his right hand in front of his face as if chasing away a fly. It was a gesture that he had adopted at some point in his life when he was practicing "mind watching." The practice involved suspending thought long enough to allow that an "answer" could be discerned in the cacophony of streaming thoughts in the mind by waving away the current conversation that Awareness was having with itself if it could be called "Awareness" when it seemed to be constructed from the patchwork of beliefs and interpretations of experience. Jimmy knew instinctively that the "present moment" stood apart from the stream of the "Mitote," the crowd of competing perceptions in the "everyday mind." Like Baba Ram Dass, Jimmy preferred to "Be Here Now," in a state Jimmy liked to call "Present Moment Awareness." This state is where Jimmy found Love.

Love, as a concept, had grown from early "proximity infatuation" - adolescent admiration of the opposite sex when it was close enough to touch - through a period when it seemed Love was something unattainable by its very nature, that nature being that Love was beyond the physical realm where Jimmy appeared to live.

Only when Jimmy pursued the idea that Love was a spiritual thing did he begin to comprehend and possibly experience that Love really could be a state of Awareness. Love, then, was beyond Time. As unreal as it sometimes seemed, Love, in some pure form in the Mind, was the only thing in life that was real - that would survive the death of the body and the lapse of the thinking that seemed to be its blood force.

As relationships continued to "fail," Jimmy continued to learn. That was another "nugget of knowledge" panned from the stream of the dream - that there were no mistakes, only different ways to approach the truth. This concept also seemed to stem the self-criticism that the Mind seemed determined to pin on him. So, Jimmy learned to wave away thoughts that weren't "useful," given that he intended to uncover the truth of love and to know this state of existence.

And then, Jenny.

Jenny had first shown up in the dream as another life force pursuing some "other world" of her imagining. She thought so, and so did he. Neither of them was actively looking for a certain future when their separate worlds seemed destined to fall apart. Indeed, that was what it seemed that the world of perception was intended to "see" - that everything in the world was subject to Time and its aging process, moving from birth to death in a slow realization of decay. The goal was to merely survive for as long as possible, keeping one's head above the surface of the vast ocean of decadence, and, if possible, to learn to swim the seas of indulgence and industriousness with some vague idea of landing on the shores of retirement and bliss, if indeed that island existed.

Then, one day, when Jimmy was eating chicken wings, Jenny walked in and said, "Hello." And that was the beginning of the end of the dream of separation, loneliness to be replaced by joining, and displacement by a sense of belonging. However, neither of them knew that when he offered her a wing.

"Jenny." Jimmy used her name to call forth that state of joined Awareness that he reveled in. "Jenny, do you remember when we first met?" Jimmy held the idea that it was when he had first become interested in her, apart from the crowd of "people passing by."

"Why, yes, Jimmy. It was at an early morning meeting when you were introduced to me."

"Not that formal introduction. I mean, when we first caught each other's attention."

"That could be when you offered me that chicken wing, Jimmy, or maybe later, really, when we danced."

Jimmy had first danced with Jenny at a mutual friend's birthday party at a local bar. They had "connected" that evening between dance and drinks and playing partners in a game of pool, sharing close conversation and casual touching. And the inkling of a dream had begun, a possibility to be explored amidst the multitude of possible scenarios to be experienced.

"You're right, Jenny. It was one or the other of those moments in Time. Unless we were always meant to be together, to live this Love and to share it by showing it. Maybe a 'Future Fate' drew us to become aware of one another."

"I don't think we'll ever know if there is an answer to that question, Jimmy. We may just have to be content that this is how it is now, without a perfect story of 'What Was' and how it became 'What Is.'"

Jimmy sighed. "Of course, you're right, Jenny. And, of course, 'Inquiring Mind' wants to 'Know.' Even if it's a made-up truth."

Jenny's laughter twinkled in the space. "You are such a genius, Boyfriend. And I'm just happy to be with you in this 'Present Moment,' where Love has not only been revealed but seems to be pouring out all over."

"Is that what's on the comforter?" Jimmy joked, realizing that "seriousness" never solved anything.

"It's gotten into everything, Jimmy! It's everywhere we look!"

"I see it, too!" Jimmy exclaimed with the same excitement. "It's everywhere we see it, there!"

"I think that's how it works, Jimmy. It just took us a while to see that."

"It was right there in front of us, too." Jimmy played on the story of how the two of them let go of all pretense of separateness.

"It still is," Jenny noted their agreement on the state of Love.

"And so it is," Jimmy said with the solemnity of a preacher invoking an "Amen."

"And so, it shall be." They said it together and turned into each other's arms.

"Maybe Love is what happens
when we quit trying to love."

143 JJ'S STORY

"Immersed in love,
life is lived without a script."

Jimmy knew that life had changed. He lived this new, certain way every day, and it wasn't what he had lived before. He didn't know much more than that. And it was enough. Everything was enough. It was all good.

Jimmy's heart sang every love song it ever knew and changed the lyrics on some to suit his new mood. Half-remembered feelings became fully fleshed. Life, once good, was now the best. And it felt like he had done nothing to allow this to unfold, and the story they told of it would never grow old. Love had boldly gone where none had gone before. And all they wanted was more of the same.

Jenny and Jimmy knew that this was something special that they shared. They knew that it had happened because they had allowed the possibility of it to enter the mind and find its way to the heart. Bodies went along for the ride. They called it "Love" because that was the closest thing they knew to explain this total immersion of one soul with another. And they danced like neither had ever danced before. And it was all good. Everything was grand.

"Jenny, do you think we'll ever be able to describe this love that we share?" Jimmy loved asking questions that couldn't be answered easily. And he loved sharing everything with Jenny.

"We'll just keep trying, Jimmy, and see what comes up!"

Jenny grinned so brightly that Jimmy forgot what he was going to say next. They had made love last night unexpectedly, and his mind was a little fuzzy from it, it seemed. It always seemed that the mind left the room when they made love. What remained was a pure awareness that thrived and throbbed with love.

"I love you, Jenny!" This was Jimmy's "fallback" statement when his mind went blank. He said it a lot. Love paused his mind all the time, took him out of time, and left him wondering. It felt amazing.

"I love you, Jimmy!" Jenny kept grinning. She could barely ever stop.

Life had morphed into a joyful stream of moments stitched together with "I love you." It felt amazing.

"That's my story,
and I'm sticking to it!"

144 JJ'S WAGON

*"Love is as real
as we make it."*

While sitting alone in the darkness of his home, he wrote a poem. It wasn't too great, but most people could relate, adding lines of their own.

Jimmy believed that he had learned to tap into the flow of life, and though it wasn't really surfing, he was riding a slow wave through an ocean of love.

It was an amazing dream, made of moments that streamed and gave semblance to time spent together or apart, here or there, when or then. And everything was Zen - guided more by feel than by thought - by the flow of love not the call of logic.

Jimmy had always thought himself smart, but it wasn't until he acknowledged that he really knew nothing at all that he began to believe that he truly knew something about life. There had been much to unlearn.

As Jimmy let go of more and more belief systems, the speed of life seemed to increase at first, like Calvin and Hobbes flying downhill in a toy wagon, then it slowed, the wagon floated, and life flew by slowly as a dream - liquid and languid, sensual and warm.

And then, Jenny.

Jenny first seemed to be a part of that same dream, flowing with an unmistakable rhythm of her own, and he was attracted to her style, her cadence, and the confidence with which she walked through life. Jimmy wondered if he could be dreaming. Some things were repeating, and others had completely changed, like a déjà vu within a dream.

As their dreams merged, Jenny knew that Jimmy was the One - much like Neo in the Matrix movies, Jimmy was learning to follow his promptings - and Jenny could see that it was good and jumped on for the ride.

"Jimmy, how do you know which are the good promptings and which are maybe not so good?" Jenny knew that Jimmy loved to talk, especially about philosophy. She cast out this line to see what she might reel in.

"Jenny! It's simple, Girlfriend. Notice if the prompting moves awareness in the direction of love and joy. If it does, it's legit. Otherwise, don't touch it."

"What if I'm feeling prompted to jump your bones, Boy?"

"Then, by all means, follow that prompting!"

And they both did.

> *"Sometimes, following*
> *looks like leading."*

145 JJ'S REFRAIN

"The song sings itself,
asking us to join."

Jimmy's father liked to sing. Although typically soft-spoken, he was inspired to sing loudly, often on a Sunday morning when Jimmy just wanted to sleep in. Maybe that was part of the prompting. From "The Sound of Music" to "My Fair Lady," many lyrics had become part of Jimmy's reckoning as if imprinted in some patterned filter for his mind. Now, Jimmy sang the same songs, and his father's legacy lived on.

Jimmy softly brushed the hair from her closed eyes and tucked it behind her ears. He reveled in the soft curve of her cheek, the line of her brow and chin, and the rise of her lips, soaking them all in, imprinting them in his eyes and heart.

"The way to handle a woman..." The song from his silent past bubbled up into awareness. "... is to love her... simply love her... merely love her... love her... love her." And Jimmy did love her in every way that he knew. He closed his own eyes for a moment, allowing love to fall softly down into his heart, like a spring snow covering all his memories of loss or ache, blanketing them to never be seen again. Love really was so simple - allow no separation. The mind always looked to define and divide, while the heart joined, adding love upon love as it looked upon One World.

"Oh, what a beautiful morning..." Jimmy sang it with open joy, but not too loudly, as Jenny pulled her awareness from dreams sleeping to love waking. "Oh, what a beautiful day..."

Jenny stretched her arms over her head and her toes towards the foot of the bed, yawning the next line, "I've got a beautiful feeling..."

They sang the refrain together softly: "Everything's goin' our way."

They tended to change any "my" lyric to "our," reinforcing the lack of separation. They told each other everything. They shared everything, from bites of peanut butter toast to shower scrubs to mowing the lawn or walking hand-in-hand downtown. Life was meant to be shared and they were living it well.

Jimmy chuckled and brushed his fingers across her chest, relishing the softness there. "Ready for coffee, my Princess?"

Jenny yawned again, "Of course I am. But first, this Princess has to pee - just like the fairy tale."

"Mmm," Jimmy considered, "I don't remember the fairy tale that way, but..." He paused and tickled her ribs lightly, "It works for me!" He rolled and jumped out of bed, brandishing his arm as if he held a sword. "I'm off to save a damsel in distress!" He pulled an imaginary cape around his torso. "I shall return! With coffee, no less!"

Jenny shook her head as she watched his retreating. She loved this man and his singing and coffee-bringing, how he seemed to always be thinking of her, even texting at perfect times to remind her how he loved her in return. 'Another beautiful day,' she thought to herself as she slid her legs off the edge of the bed and landed lightly on the rug, there. She wrapped the soft river of robe around her, the one that Jimmy had given her last Christmas. 'Or was it the Christmas before?' She hummed to herself as she walked to the bathroom, then sang a little as she crossed the hall, just loud enough for Jimmy to hear over the sound of brewing coffee: "Blue skies, smiling at me..."

He sang back from the kitchen, "Nothing but blue skies, do I see!"

'God, I love this man!' She thought as she stood in the mirror.

'God, I love this woman,' he thought. 'She is such a mirror of me!'

"All the sounds of the earth are like music..."
~ "Oh, what a beautiful morning!"
lyric by Rodgers & Hammerstein

146 JJ'S CONSIDERATION

"Love One Another."

There wasn't much about religion that Jimmy could admire. It seemed to have morphed into some ritualistic way to control the behavior and the mind of its constituents. Maybe it had always been this way. Maybe not. But the whole thing seemed to have moved away from Love as the center of existence. All the rest was just context.

Jimmy had studied "New Age" thoughts and found most of them a bit "wanting" also. Sure, the Mind was intrigued for a while by intricate belief systems and even simpler ones, like the Law of Attraction. But Jimmy finally realized that all belief systems were limiting and slowly let them all fall away (mostly), keeping a little of this or that which illuminated the One Great Truth that it was "All About Love."

Some philosophies enumerated that very thing but failed to allow it to be all-pervasive. The Beatles expressed it again and again in their songs - "Love is All There Is." Jimmy recognized that life had been leading him to remember this truth and to employ it in his life unencumbered by dogma or its derivatives. He had given away all of his "spiritual" books when he realized that there was only One Truth that they all pointed toward Love.

But knowing the Truth and living the truth were two very different things...

Jimmy's mind got in the way all the time. Even though he had trained himself to stay alert to its machinations, he fell to the power of habitual thinking often: upset at traffic and other drivers (as if he had somewhere to go and something to do in time), complaining about the "fairness" of the actions of others (as if that had anything to do with his own life or actions), wondering about the origins of creation (as if 'knowing' anything could improve his outlook on life). Jimmy just kept on swimming the vast ocean of imagination and wonder, going under at times but always rising with a new breath and zest for life as he shook water (and thoughts) from his head and gulped life.

Yes, Jimmy had learned that life was just about living and loving. And that's all he wanted to do, Now.

"Jenny." Jimmy grinned every time he turned his mind and thoughts towards her, realizing that the very idea of "Jenny" had come to represent Love in his life. "Jenny, I wonder sometimes about how everything just seems to work out."

"Jimmy, you're overthinking again." Jenny often reflected what Jimmy was thinking, a mirror to his mind.

"Well, of course I am, Jenny! That's what 'I' do." Jimmy mangled the tense purposefully. "'I' is what I think I am." He laughed, and Jenny joined in.

"'I' think you're right, Jimmy!" They laughed more.

"'I' wouldn't have it any other way!"

"'I' concur."

When they settled from laughter just a little, Jimmy continued with his original thought. "If we don't think about it, everything seems to unfold on its own most delightfully." He turned to face Jenny again, looking for recognition and understanding. "Don't you think?"

"I DO think, Jimmy. But I try not to!" Jenny knew exactly what Jimmy's words pointed towards.

"Yes. I think. It does."

"That's it, of course!" Jimmy agreed. "It's just difficult sometimes to quit thinking ahead as if that could help anything turn out one way or another. I've been thinking all my life, and I can't seem to turn it off."

"Jimmy." Jenny softened the tone of her response. "You're right about that - thinking never solved anything. Or helped much, either. 'Knowing' the truth seems to happen when thinking stops."

"Life doesn't stop when we stop thinking, Jenny," Jimmy stated this as a fact, not a question. "Thinking seems to 'be' as if it is 'who we are,' but we can stop thinking, and we're still here."

"And the best part, Jimmy, is that when we stop thinking, Love shines brighter!" Jenny said excitedly.

"I Love that about you, Gifford!"

"Gifford?"

"Well, I meant to say 'Girlfriend,' but my mind messed it up."

"That does happen, Boffo!"

"Yes. I think. It does."

"Joy happens
where thinking ends,
and Love begins."

147 JJ'S NAME

"What's in a name?
It's just how we play mind games."

Jimmy had always liked his name. It was simple enough and people seemed to remember it and him, although the two might not be related. There were other reasons that he might be remembered: a little too tall or loud, perhaps too smart or smart-ass, sometimes crass, funny (he thought he was funny), and he could tell a fairly good story. Sometimes, people used his name as a verb, like "Jimmy something open," or a noun, like "he drives a Jimmy." That always felt sort of weird, like his name didn't really describe him all that well or that he was definitely more than just a name. Mostly, he liked it, answered to it, and called himself by it.

Jenny had often thought that she would have liked a more "exotic" name, like "Wanda" or "Harper," something that couldn't be shortened easily and that stood out just a little. Jenny knew that she was more unique than her name purported. It was also inconvenient when it was shortened - then it sounded like a drink or a card game. And if someone said "next-gen," she always took it personally. Still, she kept using the name given to her. She had grown up with it, grown used to it, and could probably outgrow any menial association with it.

"Jenny," Jimmy said her name with reverence and more than a little awe as it called forth a feeling of spiritual surrender and miraculous serendipity for him. "Jenny, I've often wondered if I'd have grown up different with a different name. My mom almost called me 'Bruce,' I know. That would have changed everything, right?"

Jenny looked at Jimmy and smiled. His name rose in her heart first, and then the joy associated with it slowly spread to her face. Sometimes, she could feel it light up her entire being. "Jimmy, I think you'd have been 'Jimmy' no matter what your name was." That sounded funny, and they both laughed.

"You're such a 'Jenny!'"

"Jimmy Dahling!"

"But would you have fallen in love with me if I was 'Theodore?'"

"You'd be my 'Teddy Bear.'"

"How about 'Maximilian?'"

"I'd be mad about 'Max.'"

OK. Something harder. Like 'Cletus.'"

"That would be unique. I might have to change my name to 'Cleopatra' to be able to love you with that name!"

"Ah, Jenny, you know how much I love you?"

"I think so, but go ahead and tell me again."

"I'd love you no matter what your name was, even 'Maude.'"

"Well, Bart, I'd love you right back!"

"Thank Goddess!"

"Now, give me some 'Jimmy,' boyfriend!"

"Oh, you're gonna get some, all right."

"A rose by any other name..."

148 JJ'S FALL

"Always, This."

Jimmy had never truly been able to find "why" he was alive. He just was. Everything just started when he awoke and fell away when he laid down the day. He was "reborn" again and again, each copy slightly different as if "re-faxed," words getting more and more blurred with each repetition, everything on the page beginning to look more and more alike. Yet here he was, old enough to be grandfather a billion times, happier than he had ever been, as far as he could remember. The memory of the "past" was also blurring. "Now" seemed to be the main play of every seemingly single day. Strangely, the lack of "different" became the mainstay of how he lived - Love really was "All there Is."

Jimmy smiled when he recalled the famous Sherlock Holmes quote: "When you have eliminated the impossible, whatever remains, however improbable, must be the truth." After chasing Love down every rabbit hole imaginable, the only thing left to know was that Love is All of It. That's all that was left.

Jenny reminded Jimmy what Love looked like, felt like, sounded like. "If it looks like a duck, swims like a duck, and quacks like a duck, then it probably is a duck." In this case, it was more. Jimmy had never loved a duck.

Jenny symbolized everything good in life: companionship, friendship, spirit, communion, Love. It was All just expressions of the "One Love." The Bob Marley song and mantra had become real to Jimmy. Joy had become his song.

110

"Jenny!" Jimmy called out her name as if invoking the universe to materialize Love. "Jenny! I love you!"

Jenny rolled her face into her pillow. "It's early for that, isn't it?" Her response was muffled.

"Yes, but it's time to 'make love' and make the world!"

"You've been up for a while, haven't you?" Jenny rolled to her back. "How much coffee have you had?"

"Just enough," Jimmy responded. "Are you ready for a cup? It's hot and tasty, and I have it right here!"

"Can I pee first?"

When Jenny returned to bed, she shed her robe and backed up to the edge of the mattress. She was short, and the bed was tall, so this worked well to hoist herself up backward. Jimmy watched, fascinated by every move of her body. When she had arranged the pillows in a stack and slid back up against them, she sighed. Jimmy was like an eager puppy. He scooted closer and put his arms around her. "Mmm mmm, good!"

"I love you, too, Jimmy!" Jenny grinned at the boy's joyful expression. "Did someone mention coffee?"

"Right here, Jenny." Jimmy handed her the cup.

"Elixir of the gods!" Jenny joked, taking the first sip of the day.

"You are my Goddess, Girlfriend!"

"If that comes with coffee every morning, I'm in!" Jenny's laughter sparkled.

"As you like it." Jimmy quipped. "I'm just here to serve."

"Worshiped, I think, Jimmy. The way you treat me."

"I wouldn't have it any other way."

"When all else falls away,
Love is what remains.
Keep falling."

149 JJ'S PHILOSOPHY

"The Power of Positive Thinking positively works!"

As much as Jimmy had learned to have a positive outlook on life and to love everyone (sort of), he still complained about "their driving." Of course, he knew that even this was one more way that his mind was pointing out to him the places that still might need a little work, given that not all of Jimmy's perceptions were "loving" and didn't "fit" with his overall stated intentions. Jimmy still cussed when he stubbed his toe or hit his thumb, although sometimes he was able to alter his reactions into a sort of "self-deprecating" humor. When he didn't manage that, he went for a band-aid. And sympathy. Both were reliable ways to begin the healing process.

Unfortunately, he often forgot the "pause for the cause" that might allow him to wave away the practiced response and substitute a different one. Jimmy had become comfortable with the way he was and the way things were, and going with the flow of that seemed to be generally happy... as long as he remembered to laugh.

Jimmy had always liked to laugh. He had noticed at a very early age that people enjoyed it when you laughed at their jokes and would often join in laughter, which always felt good. Jimmy learned to laugh a lot. It was a great way to get approval even though he was a bit "unique," as Mom put it, and might even laugh too loud at times. As he gained notoriety for his laughter, Jimmy learned to appreciate that aspect, too. Not to mention that the more he laughed, the more he filled with glee as the "Mary Poppins" song went. Laughing, it turned out, was perhaps the best philosophy that he could've adopted! Laughter fits the highest aspects of most belief systems - "follow your joy," "choose happy in the dream," or even "happy is as happy does." And being joyful seemed to be reflected in his body most of the time, except for the random cuts and bruises, aches and pains, mostly associated with past belief systems that included "getting old" or "this, too shall pass."

"Jenny!" Jimmy always said her name with joy bubbling up. Jenny had taken his happiness to new levels and even the thought of her in his life brought a smile. "Jenny, I'm so glad that you're in my life! As a matter of fact, I'm 'positive' about it!" Jimmy wrote a plus sign on his chest to indicate that the positive lived in his heart.

"Jimmy! I love you, too! Isn't it great!" Jenny beamed with the joy of love, and Jimmy found his grin stretching across his face.

"It IS great!" Jimmy concurred. "Do you know how long we've been together now? And still, our love keeps growing!"

"I never thought it was possible to love this way, Jimmy! Or to be this happy!"

"I think maybe because we've both chosen this, that's why we're so joyful. It really is amazing!"

"Yes, Jimmy, you are amazing!" Jenny smiled as she turned on her "reflective mode."

"I see what you did there, Jenny." Jimmy pointed to her face. And I see the same reflection right there!"

"It's a circular argument, Jimmy."

"But we never argue!"

"Exactly! So, keep that smile on your face, and kiss me!"

"I love you, Jenny," Jimmy said and leaned in to melt in her gaze and kiss her lips. 'God, she could kiss!' he thought as he closed his eyes for the final two inches.

"God, he can kiss!" Jenny thought, closing her eyes, for the last two inches."

"Shared joy
is the best joy!"

150 JJ'S JOINT

"What do you dream about?
Me, too!
Let's go together!"

Jimmy believed in synchronicity, serendipity, and destiny, with a little "as it should be" thrown in. These were his favorite stories. They acknowledged the idea that although life arises on its own, there could be some "co-creation" at work as well. There were, after all, stories in which his actions seemed to align with the intention of the universe.

He was supposed to meet a girl at a Starbucks on Rainbow Boulevard that morning. They had never mentioned which one. He had driven past the first three without stopping. The fourth was on his right. He took that as a sign - one which he had imagined - that when he looked through his right eye, he saw the future. He pulled in and parked. She was there, of course. They talked over a latte - what Jimmy considered his "minimum investment" of time and money - and didn't really hit it off. Then she said, "I think you're supposed to meet my friend!" And led him on a drive across town - he never lost her - to park at her friend's home. When they went inside (the door was open), she called out to her friend. Jimmy said, "She's off to the left, somewhere." She emerged from the kitchen to the left and stopped in front of them. "Are you Magic?" she asked. They lived together for a number of months.

Jimmy had always had strong déjà vu experiences, mostly from dreams. He had awakened from a dream of a "square silo" once, and he had marked the dream as a "future déjà vu." He knew he would see it again someday through a series of seeming coincidences - a salesman, a Canadian, and an Italian dream - Jimmy found himself accepting a job as a superintendent building a hotel tower, something he had never done before. Some months in, Jimmy climbed to the top of the elevator shaft form and was struck with that same image from his dreams - where he stood was atop a square silo!

Jenny was one such dream, although he hadn't known it at the time they first met.

The committee was to meet to discuss hotel options for the upcoming convention. Jimmy wanted to meet at one of the options (that seemed logical to him.) But the Committee Chair had other ideas, so Jimmy went first to the venue that he had been prompted to suggest, knowing he could then catch up to the rest of the committee and have something to report. He surveyed the place and decided to check out the food at the bar, ordering dry rub chicken wings (a favorite). He had just started eating them when she walked in.

"What are you doing here?" Jimmy managed while swallowing the wing he was eating.

"I thought you were right!" she said.

Jimmy was right. And so was Jenny. And it was almost summer.

Jimmy and Jenny were watching the movie "Serendipity" together. Jimmy had seen it many times, being enthralled by the love story that happened quite by accident and the ultimate chase of the mind for "that which was meant to be." Jimmy had proposed the movie because he wanted to share his dreams of how the world unfolded perfectly, just the way it had done for them. And the movie ended happily, just as he imagined that theirs would. Had he imagined it that way? Had she? Maybe it was a joint dream, like in the movie? Maybe life was a movie. Or a dream...

"Jenny," Jimmy said her name as if he had dreamed it that way, the resonance of it tickling his throat, his heart, and his mind. "Jenny,

I just want to say that life 'AJ' is better than life 'BJ.' You know what I mean?"

"AJ?"

"After Jenny."

"Yes, life 'After Jimmy' is better than 'Before Jimmy'! And I do know!"

"I see what you did there."

"You dreamed it that way."

"We did, didn't we?"

"And now, the dream goes on."

"It's a happy dream."

> *"Which came first:*
> *Life?*
> *Or the Dream of Love?"*

151 JJ'S BODY

*"Bodies can seem
the most real part of the dream."*

Jimmy appreciated the ache from using muscles that hadn't been used for a while. Having a "project" in front of him kept his mind busy figuring out what he needed: parts, tools, and time. Home Depot workers were starting to know him by name. And working his muscles keep him busy likewise: bandaids, ibuprofen, and rest. On a good day, not needing any of the above felt like a win.

A "bad" day went differently: the new piping leaked, the paint got spilled, and he cut the board too short twice. And splinters happened. He was frustrated when his mind couldn't shape the world the way that he intended. "Close enough" was the mantra that he used to assuage his fears of inadequacy. And sometimes, he had to just walk away to play another day.

Whichever way the day went, in the end, his body was "spent," as if physical energy was a commodity that was only refreshed at a given rate. It seemed he could "earn" more by sleeping more, and that balance of time and effort seemed insurmountable. 'Had it always been that way?' Jimmy thought. 'When I was younger, hadn't I been able to go longer with less sleep? Even skipping a night now and then?' Jimmy knew that there was an answer in his mind that he didn't want to look at - that the body really did age. Or his mind believed it on such a deep level that he couldn't overcome it. He tried not to think about it.

Jenny and Jimmy had made the house their home. Although

Jimmy had lived there before inviting Jenny to move in, many of the changes that their lives had made had happened while they dreamed together, and the house reflected their joint agreements on the upgrades.

When it came time to move on, they both noticed that it wasn't a love of the house or the things in it that mattered - it was just being together in the space that was "all-important." They had created this space and would fashion the next place to suit, but it would be the shared time doing things together that mattered, wherever their bodies ended up.

"Jenny." Jimmy laughed as he spoke her name, joy bubbling up with the very idea of her sharing space and time with him. "Jenny, I do love how we take our mornings slow."

Jenny grinned. "That's the best part of every day, Jimmy - waking up slowly with your smiling face and good coffee!"

They both laughed and tapped their cups together as if toasting. "To the good life!" And they slowly sipped the hot elixir, feeling the warmth of it trickle down to the center, seemingly warming their entire bodies.

Mornings were the most fun. Bodies had been refreshed through the night, and no thoughts of the day of work ahead or plans of any kind took them from the present moment awareness of the space that they shared and the bodies that they carried - bodies that had grown accustomed to each other's company, the scents, and sensations that seemed natural, now, while their heads talked about how much they loved each other. Exchanging grins and dreams seemed to be the thing they enjoyed the most. Sometimes, they got so close that their bodies trembled and made love the only possible expression of the joy realized. And their minds let go, allowing the ideas of bodies to mesh and play. This, too, was their way. And it was good.

"Jimmy, I'm so glad to share every day with you!"
"It's the best, Jenny!"
"It's so amazing to me how the past has faded into so many memories as if the streaming of it were now just segments of remembered dreams."

"I feel that way, too, Jenny, as if this new way of living is the only real thing that there is. The rest was just practice sessions." They laughed and brushed fingers and toes together, minds lingering on the sensations of touch and the symbolism of love and endearment.

Jimmy turned to gaze into her eyes. "This is my body. I give it to you as a symbol of my everlasting love."

"Amen." She said.

And they kissed, gently at first and then passionately, as the gift was realized.

"Let the mind go where it will.
The body will follow."

152 JJ'S TACOS

"All those characters in your life?
You dreamed them up that way."

"I just don't like the guy. There's something about him that isn't trustworthy." Jimmy was talking to a coworker who had also seemed to experience difficulty with an individual.

"Don't you always say that 'the world is a reflection of the mind,' Jimmy? Then isn't this all in your mind?"

Jimmy had to pause to consider this. He DID say that all the time, but did it really apply in this situation that seemed to be so outside of him? Certainly, there were times that his mind went places that he typically wouldn't, given that he was using the First Agreement - "Be impeccable with your word" (from The Four Agreements by Don Miguel Ruiz) - as a guide in his "mind-watching." But his mind seemed to have a mind of its own. Jimmy laughed silently at this circular idea. He also said, "The Mind is a terrible waste." The mental gymnastics wasn't getting him anywhere. He KNEW that perception was a projection of the mind, or at the very least was an interpretation of the mind, so indeed, what he saw in this person was somehow IN his mind.

"You're right," he admitted. "Or I'm right, I guess! That trait really is a part of me. But it's one that I am working to purge. That much is true!"

Later, in traffic, Jimmy caught himself wanting to direct the flow. He paused his mind to look at the desire behind it. 'I want to be in control,' he thought, 'It's as simple as that. I wish I could control the world, but I can't, so I'm just projecting my frustration at that onto these unsuspecting drivers out there. Of course, they're not really "out there," are they? Maybe if I project positive vibes, then they'll drive better. Come on, you've GOT this. You CAN make a right turn on red!' Then Jimmy saw that this, too, was a projection of the same desire to be in control. He had no control over this world - not really - and he knew that if he could trust anything that he thought he "knew." He let go of the intention to make traffic conform to his idealistic view of it and sat back in the seat a little. 'What's a few seconds anyway?' he thought and enjoyed the rest of the ride home.

"Jenny! I'm so glad to be home!" And he always WAS glad, especially if Jenny was there already!

"Boyfriend!" Jenny called out with glee in her voice. "I've been waiting for you!"

"Just all my life!" Jimmy said, grinning, and reaching to hug her slight form. He gently pulled back after the hug. "Or was that me waiting for you to show up?" His eyes were grinning, and his mind was considering.

Jenny grinned back. "I think it was the same 'Mandatory Waiting Period,' Jimmy."

"Oh, no! Not that, again!" Jimmy pretended to moan. "This doesn't look like traffic anymore!"

"Pay no attention to the man behind the curtain... or the wheel." Jenny giggled as she played the Wizard of Oz line, adapting it to fit the conversation.

"There's no place like home. There's no place like home." Jimmy repeated the mantra and could feel the truth of it.

"You're home Now, Jimmy," Jenny reassured him. "And life is good."

"It's Goo-ood." Jimmy used his Jim Carrey voice, and Jenny laughed with him.

"You do keep me amused, Boyfriend!"

"It's my mission in life, Girlfriend."

"Well, if you stir the taco meat, I'll get a tortilla shell ready." Jenny pointed to the skillet on the stove with the spatula she had picked up.

"Your wish is my command!" Jimmy said, taking the spatula and stirring. "Or your wish is my wish or something like that."

"Silly Boy!"
"Amazing Girl!"
And the tacos were excellent.

*"Shared Intention
appears to be real in the dream."*

153 JJ'S DESERT

"Sometimes I wonder,
but mostly wonder happens."

Jimmy could still remember stories of that time when he had decided to give away all of his books and most of his movies, knowing, finally, that the search was over. Not because he had found anything but because he had finally realized that there was nothing to find. His world became freer, as if all of those ideas had been holding him down somehow, like Lilliput's lines on the giant that was life.

Jimmy couldn't escape all the belief systems that seemed to run on their own, but he could withdraw his opinion and, ultimately, his desire. The world kept happening. He woke to the truth of that every morning. It didn't "need" his input to "happen" it just kept arising. Jimmy's choice to go out or stay "home" was merely a preference of the "Observer," whoever or whatever that was. Jimmy didn't feel like that was "him," either, but another part of the flow of things. He could "observe" himself being happy. Sort of. Mostly, everything just "was" or "is" with "will be" somehow part of "now" and "then."

Mostly, Jimmy no longer tried to describe this feeling that, although life was so amazing, it was also not very real, being made of dreams and such. He wandered through it like David Carradine in Kung Fu, noticing what showed up and "dealing with it." But he was happier than Kwai Chang or believed that he was, having released most "guilt feelings" about what seemed to be his past. Jimmy thought that he might write a book about this "new" way of life if he could find the time. Or the inclination. These seemed linked, somehow.

When Jenny showed up in his life, he had been skeptical at first, having "been there done that" enough to be skeptical about everything and everyone who showed up in the dream. Yet she had put her spark to his dying embers, and the breeze that followed her seemed to fan the flame of some "past knowing" to become the source of light and joy. Perhaps Kwai Chang did not need to wander anymore. Having abandoned the search, maybe life had brought to him the very thing he had been looking for - love.

"Jenny." Jimmy spoke her name as he did his own, with a familiarity that was embedded in his very idea of "who he was."

"Jenny, do you think we'll ever know what's really going on?"

"Jimmy. You're doing it again." Jenny knew that she could join his musings or distract him from them, and either choice was valid.

"What, Jenny?"

"You're overthinking it. You told me to remind you if you were 'lost in thought,' as you didn't really want to waste any more time running down rabbit holes."

"So right, Jenny! Thank you!"

"It was nothing. Really. Nothing is going on."

"I see what you did there..." Jimmy grinned broadly.

"It was your idea, remember?"

"I suppose so."

"Too late. You already did."

"Suppose?"

"No thanks. I've already had some."

"Goddess, I love you!"

"That IS the answer to all of your questions!"

"Amen!" Jimmy reached out, pulling her into him for a kiss and a hug, the touch of her almost as intoxicating as her mind.

"No Time
IS
Play Time."

154 JJ'S MIRROR

"I read something about that.
Does that mean anything?"

Jimmy knew that "what you look at grows." When he was looking for a certain thing - maybe it was a car or a Harley - he started seeing them everywhere. It was as if the universe were responding to his thoughts about it. Now that tracking one's movements on the internet was such a thing, he often got ads on Facebook right after "searching" something (even talking about something?) - and he thought at least the Universe was responding to his thoughts about it! Maybe that's how the Universe worked, anyway, and the context of "internet tracking" was developed by the mind as a way to explain what was going on. Maybe the Universe was just being better and quicker at reflecting? Or was the mind allowing that to be true, having discarded so many thoughts to the contrary?

Was everything just context? Jimmy dared to think this at times, as it both invigorated and inebriated him. Was the story his own to make? The Dude really does abide?

They had talked about retirement. They had pointed to being somewhere warm. Jenny and Jimmy had said repeatedly that they just preferred being together. They had chosen Las Vegas for vacation trips many times. It seemed convenient to do so, given that they liked concerts and people and football. Why would it be a surprise that the Universe bent down and tapped them on the shoulder, saying, "Go there."

Life had seemed to get better and better after Jimmy had responded to the call of the Universe, pointing for him, "She's right there in front of you!" Going "All in" was a way of life now. And joy was everywhere! Maybe Jimmy had finally removed the blocks to love in his mind, and that's how he was now able to see it clearly, to know it dearly. And to live it.

It seemed that there was some work to get done, but it wasn't anything that they didn't want to do, anyway - let go of "things" that they didn't need, streamline their lives a bit to enable more time spent together, pass on what they had made in their first home together. They were spending more time just being together doing things so that they could spend more time together in the future. A good loop to be caught in!

"Jenny!" Sometimes, the very thought of her made his heart skip! "Jenny, we're really doing this!"

"It seems that way, Jimmy. All signs point to 'Yes' in the dream."

"It sometimes feels like a big move, but other times, it seems like it was inevitable, and the time frame was just sped up a little."

"I'm glad it's happening. It feels right."

"How do we know it's right?" Jimmy asked the question as part of the established interplay they had created - that they spoke in affirmations that synced with the Flow of Life.

"Because that's what's happening, Jimmy!"

They laughed together. It was the laughter that kept them together. Another affirmation of the joy of sharing love.

"We should have a party!"

"And give stuff away!"

"A party to remember, that's for sure!"

"Jimmy, we have become memorable!" Jenny laughed. "Just wear that grin, Boyfriend!"

"Grin. Check. Joy." Jimmy put his hand over his heart. "Check."

"Check it out, Jimmy!" Jenny laughed as she spoke.

"I haven't 'checked out' yet, Girl!"

"You checked me out, Boy."

"And I liked it, unh hunh, unh hunh."

"Do a little dance..."

They sang the KC & the Sunshine Band verse together, "Get down tonight!"

*"Synchronicity is
the most natural thing
in the Universe."*

155 JJ'S OPTIONS

"Love is not optional."

If there was one thing Jimmy knew, it was that most of what he thought he had known was no longer true. So many platitudes, cliches, and semi-truths that have to be unlearned. He didn't want his brow to sweat or be in the sunset; he wasn't looking to get what he gave or pave any streets with the best intentions. He had discovered something that had always been there, lying just beneath the surface of all of these miscommunications - "We're making it up as we go."

Like the Matrix movies in which an entire world is made up to keep the true self in a state of semi-consciousness, Jimmy had learned to watch his mind generate its troubles and then work hard to solve them. "Busy work."

Now, the more that Jimmy stayed "present," the easier life had become, unfolding in its almost perfect way just for him to play. How else could he explain this joyful state that he now lived in?

Jenny.

Of course, Jimmy's life had become radically more joyful with the arrival of Jenny. Jimmy hadn't been looking, really, but there she was, right in front of him, apparently (so it now seemed) just for the two of them to get to know one another. And it felt as if they had always known each other. Maybe even like they had done this all before, in different lifetimes. 'But,' Jimmy thought, 'the mind can live so many lifetimes in a single day. Maybe they just clicked so completely because the Universe wasn't random after all.'

In his mind, Jenny was a miracle. 'How could anyone seem so perfect for him?' Jimmy thought it amazing, having noticed that he was so unlike the other characters in his dream. Yet here she was. She spoke like him, ate like him, laughed and sang and danced like him, loved like him. She really was a mirror of him! There was no way Jimmy was going to mess this relationship up - no way at all.

"Jenny!" Jimmy's mind used Jenny's name like punctuation now - she was always on his mind, so it was simply a matter of considering her in all of his ideas. 'Jenny, [comma], do you want to...' - do whatever it was that his mind had come up with.

"Jenny, it's another day!"

"How long have you been up, Jimmy? And how much coffee have you had?"

"A while and some, Jenny."

"Did you forget that it's Saturday?"

"No, Jenny, that's why I'm back!"

"Ok, then. Give me a minute to finish waking up."

"I'm here to do just that, Girlfriend!"

"You are, aren't you? I like that about you, Jimmy."

"That I keep showing up every day?"

"That you enjoy your coffee."

"I brought one for you."

"That's what I'm talking about. Not only do you love the same things that I do, you want to share them, too!"

"Everything's more fun, shared. Tastes better, too."

"So, I've heard!"

"That's because you made it up that way."

"Yes, we did, didn't we."

"I love that about you!"

"That I'm agreeable?"

"That you smell good. Just kidding. That you enjoy making things up as we go. Spontaneous, you know. And you don't smell bad. That's true, too!" They laughed.

"How about we hug a little and then have coffee?"

"I thought you'd ask that!"

"Ask, and you shall receive.
Talk, and the mind will be opened."

156 JJ'S WORDS

"Please, celebrate me home
Play me one more song,
That I'll always remember..."
~ Kenny Loggins

Jimmy sometimes wondered about the power of a name. What if he called himself "James" or even "Jim?" Would his entire life have been different? He guessed it didn't matter - he was just who he was - "Jimmy" - and that worked for him.

Jimmy liked long words, too, like "callipygian," "pulchritude," or "flatulence." He remembered his Uncle coming for Christmas and always springing new words on him and his siblings. Luckily, mom had a big Merriam-Webster, and they could run to it and look up words if they could guess the spelling. Mom always had them look up words that they found in books and encouraged them to read the definitions of the words in front of and after the words that they were looking up. They learned a lot of words and meanings that way. They guessed that Uncle had read a lot of books to know all of those words.

Later, when Jimmy took Latin in high school, he found that so many words in English actually came from Latin! Some morphed a bit as they passed through the "Romance countries" - countries that were part of the Empire of Rome - France, Italy, Spain, and some others. Words were combined or took on local flavor and spelling. Jimmy found it fascinating! He learned more English from Latin than he did taking English Lit! Later, Jimmy learned that people used words to hold things in place, and really old words held the oldest ideas firmly, so that the mind could accept the truth of them and point to what they meant, and everyone would agree. A tree is a tree, after all.

It was either reading about existentialism or quantum theory that had Jimmy doubting even that idea. Maybe a tree was whatever he wanted it to be...

With Jenny, Jimmy learned the true meaning of communication - "to make One by sharing all." The Latin etymology boiled down to something like that, and relationship defined it even better. He and Jenny shared everything. This led to them being close in perspective - they were already that when they met - and also completely trusting - which led to complete intimacy. It was natural that they could complete each other's sentences as their thought trains left from the same station.

Jimmy had read more, but Jenny listened better. Together, they had formed their world of ideas and purpose. What else was there to do?

"Jenny." Jimmy knew that her name pointed to an entire universe of thought and feeling, and he spoke it reverently as such. "Jenny, do you realize that we've become closer than many couples ever do? Maybe more than most?"

"It sure feels that way, Jimmy. I think it's because we don't hold anything back from each other."

"That isn't always an easy thing to do, is it?"

"Not in my experience. You know that we've seen some couples that seem as happy as we do, but it isn't all that common."

"Well, it hasn't been all that common in my past lives either!" Jimmy laughed, and Jenny joined him, recognizing the truth in the statement.

"Things were different. We used to have different priorities, like raising children and walking the dog."

"Neither of which is easy, Jenny!"

"Our responsibilities have changed, Jimmy. We are now more concerned with our happiness."

"That sounds sort of harsh, Jenny, but it's true. And since, for both of us, our main concern is our joy, life gets better and better!"

"I love you, Jimmy!" And she meant what she said, and Jimmy understood the truth behind the words.

"I love you, too, Jenny." And he leaned close to share a kiss. His body trembled a little as he focused on the exchange.

"Now, that's communication!"

And they both laughed and kissed.

"To become One,
there can be no walls."

157 JJ'S MILIEU

*"Life's a big surprise
You with the stars in your eyes
Love has no disguise."*

Jimmy had never felt quite this way before. Life was much more fun now that he'd become "All in." If any old buttons were pushed, he mentally repeated that verse - "all in" - and it kept things from getting worse. Jimmy knew the mind could run away with its thoughts and go places that it hadn't ought, but his mind training kept his head above that course. He had been there, done that, and had no desire to repeat any of it. When he "stayed the course" of love, all things smoothly sailed, and the winds blew warm and steady.

This Love that they both had found was something special. They didn't have to try to "make a go" of it. It flowed so naturally it was as if they had always been together. Maybe they had.

"I've been waiting... for someone new... to make me feel alive." The song lyric from Foreigner had been waiting for them to find each other, it seemed. Together, now, life made more sense, and so did every love song ever written - the happy ones anyway.

It felt like life sang now for Jimmy, as if by giving himself over to the magic of love, all of life became magical! It made sense, he guessed. 'And to think I once pushed this chance away...'

"Jenny." Jimmy's voice held a tenderness in it that even he had never known before, as if calling her name invoked the power of heaven on earth. "Jenny, it's Monday. The weekend's over."

Jenny replied, "Mmmphh," with her face in her pillow, then raised her head to look at the light coming in through the window.

"Do we hafta?" She said and dropped her head back to the pillow.

"Well, neither of us is ready to retire just yet. So, I guess, yes, we 'hafta.' I brought coffee."

Jenny pulled herself into a sitting position, fluffing the pillows up against the head of the bed. "Did you say, 'coffee,' Boyfriend?"

Jimmy handed her the drink. Jenny took it carefully. "It's hot," Jimmy said.

"Yes." Jenny tipped the cup to her lips and sipped. "It feels so good going down, like it warms my entire body as it makes its way to my toes!"

"No reason to stop at the stomach that I can think of." Jimmy quipped.

"Alien anatomy," Jenny replied.

"I knew this was too good to be true in human terms."

"Other-worldly, my Boy. The world we knew before couldn't hold the two of us!"

"That's it!" exclaimed Jimmy. "We're in a parallel universe!"

"One of our own making, Jimmy."

"That explains everything!"

"Or nothing at all."

"Well, there is that possibility, but my mind would rather hold on to the idea that it knows something than admit that it knows nothing at all."

"Sigh," Jenny said the word and acted it out. "But at least we have each other."

Jimmy nodded. "And that's all I need to know."

"There's nowhere on earth that I'd rather be..."

They sang the last line together: "than holding you, tenderly."

"Life is meant to be a love song."

158 JJ'S RIDE

"In your eyes,
I see Love realized."

Jimmy seemed to have gotten love "wrong" all his life. Whatever the reasons, what began as "love" turned into something like passive acceptance, less passion, and less pleasure than he had imagined "being in Love" to be. It may have simply been a "reaction" to losing his first love unexpectedly and the pain that carried with it. Maybe Jimmy had been holding something back ever since, experiencing only what his heart dared to risk in a self-fulfilling, prophetic pattern of pathetic purpose. How could he experience "Love" with a capital "L" when he wasn't willing to "go there"?

Jimmy had married for "Love" and divorced for the same reason. When passion faded and interest waned, his mind wandered and took his heart along for the ride. 'Maybe there is no such thing as "True Love"; maybe that was always just a fractured fairy tale,' Jimmy thought.

And the older he got, and the more relationships that he entered (and left or lost), the more that idea prevailed.

Then, Jenny.

At first, Jimmy thought, 'Here we go again.' The pattern seemed to be set, and he recognized the probable hurt before it could be realized. He pushed her away. The story was too similar to his "last, best" relationship. And that hadn't ended well. Not at all.

But his dog had died, and the house had gotten really quiet, so he reconsidered, sitting in the dark alone. He looked at a picture of Jenny on his phone. She reminded him of his first wife and a little like his first love in high school. Maybe the Universe was conspiring with his mind to do just that - mimic the "look of love" so that he would mindlessly fall once more. 'Not this time,' he thought. 'She's cute and smart and smiling all the time, but that always changes.'

But it didn't. Every time she showed up, she had that same grin that looked like: "Life is meant to be fun! Won't you join me?" And the invitation seemed genuine.

And then they danced.

Jimmy had learned to like dancing. He hadn't been very good at it when he first tried it, attempting to "two-step" with a girl in Wyoming. He told her as much, and she guided him a little and then got him to "swing dance." This was genuine fun! Dancing was almost the opposite of thinking. The less he thought about it, the better he danced! And that was truly freeing. Jimmy had apparently been caught up in his "mental machinations" for far too long. He craved dancing, but, for all of his imaginings, he never found someone who wanted to dance the way that he wanted to dance - free and easy and "who cares who's watching?".

And then, Jenny.

Sure, he guided her in their first dance, instructing her to let go of thinking and just to feel the music and to let that feeling lead her. And she had, and she did, and it was good.

Jimmy was fascinated, but his heart was weary and wary. Still, he wanted to "see" her and dance with her again - was it a fluke created by good music and good alcohol? Had it been real? Usually, Jimmy could "look ahead" in time to see if a thing turned out to be part of his "future." Then, he could respond accordingly. There were signs - voices of those around him and voices in his mind - that said, "Don't go there." But he had learned to "overrule" signs before, using the "Hold my beer" mentality.

This seemed like a good plan. And the idea of Love grew as they eye-gazed and imagined, as they talked and then as they danced once again.

Years later, the dance had only become more free. And it kept
loosening each of their pasts, shaking out any remnants of sadness
embedded there, replacing old wounds with new memories and
certain trust as if love was engineering something amazing and pure.
And dance they did! Now, the music seemed to be everywhere,
inviting them to listen and play and explore a space where harmony
grew when they read the wind with their hearts.

"Jenny." Jimmy's heart always tickled a little as he said her name
because that's what she still did - tickled his heart to laugh with love.
"Jenny, this life is just so amazing! Thank you for joining with me!"
"Thank you, too, Jimmy! It's been a great ride so far!"
"Magic carpet ride!"
"Probably better than that!"
"Close your eyes, Girl. Look inside, Girl. Let the sound take you
away!" Jenny joined him in singing the well-known lyrics to the
Steppenwolf song. That was something else they did together as if
they had grown up listening to the same music on the wind, recalling
the words and the feelings that went with them, and sharing both.
"Well, you don't know what we can find..." They broke out
laughing. They didn't care how they sounded or if the words were
even right, just that they felt this way - open, trusting, free to be.
That's what Love had become - a dance of hearts and minds that
twined their souls.
"That's what I'm talking about, Girlfriend!" Jimmy blurted
breathlessly. "That's it exactly!"
"Whatever do you mean, Sir?" Jenny responded coyly, using her
southern accent to feign demureness.
Jimmy tickled her ribs in response, and Jenny laughed and brushed
away his hands. "Ah, Jenny! We are so much alike. Like the colors of
the rainbow - we share much in common, even though we are
different in many ways, too. The hues of our life together blend to
form something beautiful, and everyone can see it and feel it."
"They can, can't they." Jenny dropped the accent to acknowledge
the tone of Jimmy's oration. "And all we do is just love each other
completely."
"Without reservations. Unless we're going out to dinner."

"You always make those reservations, Boyfriend."

"I've made them all my life. But you've taught me to drop them and go 'All in' for love."

"Free falling, Jimmy. We both are."

Jimmy started singing. "Well, you don't know what we can see..."

Once again, Jenny joined him. "Why don't you tell your dreams to me. Fantasy will set you free..."

"Love is freedom in expression."

159 JJ'S MUSE

"It does seem extreme
To believe it's all a dream
Nothing's as it's seen."

As far as Jimmy knew, he had always "been," and he would "be" as long as he would "be." What else was there but his perceptions to rely on? Everything else seemed to come and go, like some sort of show that he could watch and feel and never "know." When he looked at the possibility that anything was possible, his thoughts ran the gamut from incredulity to awe as he realized the freedom that went with that. Then his mind kicked in with all of its history of "doubt thoughts" and ideas of "fear" and "pain," and he had to literally shake his head to clear it!

'How could "I" dismiss this possibility of bliss?' Jimmy wondered. 'When I look, life had been like reading books, a story of the time it took.'

And it seemed that he was right. It seemed that he was always right. 'Maybe that's the key to all of this,' he mused. 'It's as "real" as I make it!' And he grinned while buttering his toast.

Jimmy knew that Jenny was still sleeping in the other room. He wanted to let her sleep, but he also wanted to wake her up, as his favorite way to pass through time was sharing it with her! He could recall a time "before Jenny," and he knew that he had been happy then, too, but in this "Now," his intention and attention turned towards this amazing joy that he was experiencing. The feel of it was energizing. The perception when he turned in Jenny's direction was elation. How could he ever want anything else? It was unthinkable and, therefore, not possible.

"Jenny." Jimmy typically said her name with a little sigh in his voice and his heart, as if her name alone gave life. "Jenny, I've been thinking again, and I just want you to know that just like the Pet Shop Boys song, 'You are always on my mind.'"

"Jimmy, I love it when you sing, and you always seem to be singing to me." It was Jenny's turn to sigh. "And I lose my mind around you!"

"What mind?" Jimmy quipped. "Have you seen mine anywhere around here? I lost it some time ago..."

"It seems we both have, Jimmy!"

"We'll just have to stay together until we find them again."

"Maybe I don't want to, Jimmy."

"You don't want to stay?" Jimmy asked in an amused voice, feigning shock.

"I don't want to find my mind again, you dork! You know just what I mean!" She pretended to punch his arm. "You know you're asking for it!"

"That's exactly right, Girlfriend! I'm asking for it..." He paused and made as if to pounce on her, "... and I'm gonna get it!" Jimmy did pounce on her, tickling her ribs and pretending to eat her face. He leaned his head back. "And you're gonna like it!"

Jenny faked a scream, and pretended to resist, then gave it up. "Just take me, Boyfriend!"

"Apparently, that has been my intention all along, my Dear." And he growled at her neck, then kissed it.

"Whatever do you mean, Sir?" Jenny played her Southern Belle.

Jimmy played Yosemite Sam mixed with Popeye, "I yam what I yam, and I takes what I takes."

"Well," Jenny blushed coquettishly. "Please, take your time about it!"

"I mean to do just that!" And Jimmy meant exactly that.

"Love is found
in the time it takes
to make it."

160 JJ'S MIRACLE

"Love is the Guide."

Jimmy looked over to Jenny. Jenny looked up, eyes shining and a hint of a smile on her face. It seemed like she was always smiling. Jimmy's body shuddered involuntarily. It was as if the sensing of all that love that they shared was too much for the regular nervous system to handle, and it had to release some energy to maintain a sense of equilibrium. It didn't work. Jimmy always felt as if he were falling, falling deeper into love, and there was no lifeline of past information for him to grab hold of.

But he found that he could breathe underwater! He could learn new ways of living that required little, if any, thought processes. The flow of love became easier and easier to follow, carrying him above any rocks in the river of life. He glided by feeling and knowing, with the certainty of love as his guidance.

"Jenny, I didn't used to believe in miracles and now I do."

"Jimmy, you are such a romantic!"

"I suppose that could be true, but I'm telling you the truth - us being together is like a miracle, and we fit each other so wonderfully that no one could believe it! Not even 'Past Jimmy.'"

"Well, 'Present Jenny' believes that this was all meant to be because here we are, and it is what it is!"

"That much is obvious, Girlfriend. At least, now it is."

"Now is all we have, Boyfriend."

"You even sound like me!"

"I am you, remember?"

"You're a better-looking version..."

"Well, yes, that's true! I like that you're a big, strong man..."

"And I like that you're a 'diminutive woman,' like that story from my past."

Jenny sang a verse from My Fair Lady: "He takes good care of me..."

Jimmy joined in: "Wouldn't it be loverly..."

"How do you know it's right?
It's effortless."

161 JJ'S PULSE

"Wouldn't you know it?
Love is what I have to show it."

Life always seemed to move in pulses for Jimmy. At least once, he had "left home" as a "young man" and gone out to "seek his fortune."

Isn't that how the story goes?

Jimmy chased his story from one side of the country to the other, from one job site to the next, from one crew to another, and life had remained an adventure throughout! Now, it seemed he would be circling back to an earlier dream, a consistent meme overlaid with a few new schemes.

Jimmy had changed through the years in some ways. In other ways, he was the "same old Jimmy" that he had always been.

What was different was Jenny.

Jenny now occupied much of the space of his heart and his mind and colored the time with her smile. Jimmy's life had never been so joyful! Literally, life was "full of joy" from dawn to dusk and back again! Jimmy could see no end, only new beginnings.

As life pulsed, things got left behind. A camper, a Harley, a boat, and now a house - "appearance unnecessary now." Shift happened. And life moved with it! It was time for a change of venue (evidently) just when they had gotten so comfortable with where they were at. Maybe it was because of that. Still, they were "settled in" to loving each other, and that was all that truly mattered. And good coffee every morning. And a good bed to share wherever they were.

"Jenny!" Sometimes, when Jimmy turned his attention directly on Jenny, joy just bubbled up as if her name called it forth.
"Baby, do you know what I like?"
"What?" Jenny asked, playing her part in the conversation.
"Everything!"
"You DO love everything, don't you, Boyfriend!"
"Everything that has YOU in it, Girlfriend!"
"Awww, Boy, you make me blush."
"I love it when your cheeks show a little pink!"
"Yours do, too!"
"Yikes! I just can't hide it! 'I'm about to lose control, and I think I like it!'" It did seem that all the best lines of all the love songs Jimmy had ever heard were bubbling up to match the feelings that percolated now in Jimmy's and Jenny's life.
Jenny started the next line of the Pointer Sisters song: "And I know, I know, I know, I know..." and they finished it together:
"I know I want you. I want you!"
They broke out in laughter and kisses.
Life was definitely good.

*"Laughter and Love
go hand in hand.*

*Like a young couple,
the joy never ends!"*

162 JJ'S PRAYER

"In my secret heart,
I knew that love can never part."

The sun would be up early again today. Jimmy was awakened by a bird song lilting through the open bedroom window. He had been dreaming, and the world took a few moments to settle into place. He got up, steadied his balance, walked to the window, and closed it. The air that was pouring into the room was squeezed and then cut off. Jimmy closed the shades, too, thinking that Jenny needed to sleep a wee bit more. He turned to look at her form huddled in the comforter, hair tumbling onto the pillows, and he wondered what she dreamed of. He blew her a kiss and left her to her dreams. He knew that if he tarried, staring, Jenny would feel his gaze and wake to it. Somehow, that was a part of Jimmy's waking dream.

Jimmy sipped his coffee and watched the scene slowly lighting up out the living room window. The earth had tilted quickly from winter into near summer, calling thunderstorms to follow it. Flowers had sprung up overnight, pulled by the sun's gravity to shudder in the afternoon rains. The sparrows and finches ate frantically at the feeder, joined by squirrels and mourning doves, while freshly hatched rabbits chewed at the lawn. It was a circle of life worth watching, Jimmy thought to himself. 'Made precious by the link to time.'

When Jimmy looked at Jenny's still sleeping form, he thought the same thing. 'I hope that I have lots of time to express this love.' Love had come around on its own, tilting Jimmy's world and pulling at his heart until flowers appeared there, too. 'An even greater "circle of life,"' Jimmy thought.

"Jenny." Jimmy finally aimed her name at her sleeping form. And she woke to it and rolled over, pulling some covers with her. "Jenny," Jimmy continued, "I love every day with you!"

Jenny made a noise that sounded a bit like "thenletmesleep," but it could been "I love you, too," Jimmy thought, choosing the latter translation.

"I brought coffee!"

This seemed to have a gradual effect on Jenny's awareness, entering her body to resume a day of living.

"Coffee?" She said it with a questioning tone.

"Yup," Jimmy said matter-of-factly. "Fresh ground and hot-brewed for your drinking enjoyment."

Jenny finished shaping the stack of pillows and leaned back into them. She reached her hands out to take the steaming cup and put it first to her nose to smell it, then took a cautious sip. "It's wonderful. Thank you." She kept sipping it and mumbling something that sounded like 'delicious.'

Jimmy grinned and watched her, sipping from his cup, paralleling her, sensing the same warmth flowing down into the belly of the world.

"Mmm-mmm, good," Jimmy said between sips. "Just like you!"

"Take and drink of this, for this is the blood of everlasting life." Jenny mimicked Jimmy's voice as she spoke. Jimmy almost spit his coffee with a sudden burst of laughter.

"You got me there, Girlfriend!" He conceded. "But it IS good coffee!"

"Especially because you come with it, Boyfriend!"

"And so it is," Jimmy repeated the long version of 'amen.'

"And so, it is."

"Enjoy the moment.
Life is made of them."

163 JJ'S SEASONING

"It's the season of dreams."

Almost everything that Jimmy ever read said that everything one sees is a dream. "It's all in your head." Even his mind had taken up the mantra, although that was perhaps even more self-serving than the idea that "we are making it all up as we go." Either way, Jimmy knew that he couldn't use reason and logic to predict what was next in the dream and could only rely on something as ephemeral as a feeling, an inkling, a "sign." He really did need to "lose his mind."

Jimmy's life had been on cruise control for a while, with a very long road out ahead leading nowhere in particular. Then Jenny had shown up, the universe thinking it would just toss them together and see if anything good came of it. Or maybe it was just an inkling. The idea grew on each of them until "being together" seemed more natural than being apart. That's when the flashes of light, like sudden insights, started happening.

"Jenny." Jimmy had become accustomed to having not only a partner but a best friend to bounce things off. "Jenny, did you ever wonder what's really going on around here?"

Jenny loved it when Jimmy got all philosophical and shit and was willing to share his ideas, big or small, with her. "Jimmy, I think I used to wonder, and then I gave up because wondering didn't seem very productive."

"Well, you're right, there, Girlfriend. Ditto for me. That's why I quit looking in 2008 - I realized all that looking wasn't getting me anywhere, either."

"What did you do, then, Jimmy?"

"I gave away all of my so-called 'spiritual' books and started incorporating what I thought I knew into my everyday life. Bringing the training 'home,' so to speak." Jimmy pointed to his temple to give "home" the meaning that he wanted to convey: that "it's all in the mind."

"But I think that I can feel and not think too much..." Jenny began.

"Most feelings come from thought." Jimmy pointed to his temple again. "Not the other way around."

"Are you sure about that, Jimmy?" Jenny questioned his ideas on a regular basis, being not only his "Muse," but also his "check and balance."

"I'm pretty sure that when I stop thinking, the only feelings that I have are like that Eagles song - 'peaceful and easy,' Girlfriend."

"Well, that's a feeling, too, and it didn't require thinking."

"Well, the 'idea' of 'peaceful,'" - Jimmy emphasized - "could only be known by thinking. So that feeling could only be known by the 'idea' of it. Otherwise, there would just be a state of 'stasis.' Don't you think?" Jimmy laughed at his ironic comment.

Jenny laughed with him. "Perhaps Thou dost think too much," she quipped.

"Dost I?"

"Yes. And it's very self-defeating."

"My desired goal, exactly!" Jimmy exclaimed. "If there was a 'self' to do anything." He grinned broadly, eyes and face in sync.

"Well, I like your 'self' and my 'self,' Boyfriend. Especially when they're together."

"Me, too, Jenny, if there is..."

Jenny interrupted. "Oh, there's a 'me,' all right." She reached for him and tried to tickle him. "And this 'me' is all over 'it!'" They both laughed.

Jimmy turned his body in towards hers. "And that's a nice reflection on 'me,'" he joked and then kissed her.

"Just who do you think's doing the kissing?"

"It's just my imagination, running away with 'me'..." Jimmy sang the Temptations lyric and burst out laughing. "Ahh, the Mind is such a terrible wasteland."

"Walk, don't run."
"I'm in."

*"One can't
love too much,
but can certainly
think too much."*

164 JJ'S SPRING

"Spring brings back
the wonder of things."

Jimmy had always loved walking in the park, following the trails through flower beds, trees blossoming with leaves, and the grass growing longer faster than it could be mowed. Maybe it was the promise that life would always arise again, no matter how harsh the winter or how long. Maybe his eyes and everyone else's were programmed to respond to color, and the bright green had grown to be representative of the miracle of rebirth, with pops of yellow and blue and red punctuating that bright field like the best stories.

The walks would get even more precious as the time to move approached. These gardens that he had grown so accustomed to walking each year would be left behind for other, different paths and plants.

"In the room, the women come and go, Talking of Michelangelo." Funny, that line from a distant J. Alfred Prufrock poem crossed the path of his thinking as if called forth by his very melancholy.

"There will be time, there will be time.
To prepare a face to meet the faces that you meet..."

And Jimmy wondered that in the great desolation of thought and past remembrances, the ideas of time and place might be the consistent backdrop to living, this moment and then this, and who will show up to share a conversation, and when and where.

Then he shook his head to clear it and went looking for his love.

He took Jenny's hand as they walked, just as he had a thousand times before and hopefully thousands more hence, and they talked of many things, of why the winter had gone long, and "what's that bug with wings?" The grass seemed greener, shared, and flowers brighter, and they took turns pointing and trying to remember what to call each one, as if the name, the knowing, would make them shine the more. And they walked.

"Jenny," Jimmy said matter-of-factly, as he had grown accustomed to her presence in his life at his side. "Jenny, do you know what day it is?"

"Today?" Jenny grinned. She loved to tease the boy just as he loved teasing her.

"That," he said, "and it's the anniversary of our walking through this park for the umpteenth time, just before your birthday."

"I remember it well," Jenny quipped, playing her part in the game in the exchange.

"Of course you would, Girlfriend! After all, it IS your birthday!" Jimmy enjoyed making fun of his mind by saying impossible things and picturing his many dreams, stories to be painted on the many backgrounds, worlds without borders, it seemed.

"But not for a few days." Jenny pointed to the obvious flaw in his thinking. "But it's close enough, I suppose."

And they both grinned as they walked and pointed, marveling at how life came springing back each year.

"Just this.
It all points to this moment.
Choose 'happy' in the dream."

165 JJ'S CHORUS

"I try not to have any new ideas of my own.
The Universe seems to have me covered there."

Jimmy knew a few things about a lot of things and a lot about a few things, but seeing that it really came from nothing was really something and very freeing.

Amazingly, the shift began just when love started to color everything. Maybe it was because of that? Love washed his mind and lapped at the shores of his soul like some great ocean pulling him from the sands of his past, expecting him to dive in and swim. And dive, he did.

Jenny swam with him, her side stroke smoother than his, maybe more practiced.

'It's a good thing everybody floats in the ocean!' Jimmy thought and then realized that was exactly what was happening! Love buoyed him, carried him, sustained him, and all he had to do was swim.

Jimmy rolled over in bed and touched her sleeping body. Somehow, the sensation of touch made everything seem more real. Jenny stirred when he touched her, which accentuated the "reality" of it, cause and effect being an idea that the mind gleefully held on to as it sustained its belief in itself.

"Are you awake, Jenny?"

"Well, I wasn't, but I am now." She rolled her body towards Jimmy, welcoming his touch.

"I brought coffee and conversation!"

"Maybe I'm still dreaming..."

"Your prince has arrived!"
"How could a girl ever get so lucky?"
"Or a man?"
"Jimmy, you're my best dream ever."
"Ditto, Girlfriend! Now it's time to sit up and sip up!"
"... and a poet, too!"
"Roses are red, violets blue. I'd get up if I were you!"
"Silly Boy!"

"We write the lyrics
to our own songs."

166 JJ'S MATH

*"The Mind is
a terrible wasteland."*

Jimmy knew that thinking had not ever "produced results" in this world but had always come "after the fact."

'Life arises, and the mind tries to describe it, name it, and claim it!' He thought this much was true even though it arose from thinking, too. 'Yet, I am called to "Do," to exert effort to accomplish things, to sweat, to try, to wonder why... What is it that drives me by past thoughts about the way the world works? It's a "line of thinking," a linear equation of cause and effect which the mind has deemed to be true. I am the cause of my own demise,' Jimmy thought.

"This Love that we share, Jenny, is the best thing ever! It has been freeing to be 'all in' for love because if the mind starts to judge - and it lives to judge - then I can point to my heart," Jimmy pointed to his heart, "and say, 'I'm all in,' and the mind has to give in and give up. The heart really can lead the mind!"

Jenny looked at Jimmy, listening with her heart open and her eyes smiling. She loved all the ways that Jimmy expressed his love, and this was a really good one!

"Jimmy, your mind is big but not as big as your heart." She reached and lay her hand on his chest. "I can feel that."

"Jenny," he reached his hand to rest over her heart, "and your love is bigger than all the rest of you!" He laughed and Jenny took up the laughter with him.

"Jimmy, this love is so good that it encompasses all of the thinking that we have done in the past or just yesterday, and it shines bright in the mind of tomorrow!"

"That's it, isn't it, Jenny! Linear thinking has been disrupted! There is no timeline, just a pool of time circling the ageless center of love."

"We're swimming in it." Jenny offered.

"Soaking in it," Jimmy added, sighing.

"Can we add bubbles?"

"I think we already have, Darling!"

> *"And it was Friday,*
> *which is almost always*
> *very good."*

167 JJ'S DICE

"Our two lives have meshed
This One is the best yet!
Love is glad we met."

Once upon a time, in a life far, far away from this one, a boy and a girl were living completely separate lives. They each had dreams and gentle musings played on historic strings, lives like music on the wind. Then, one day, some notes collided, life coincided, gently new futures were decided. Now, the fairy tale is true; there is nothing left to do except go where they're guided.

"Jenny." The vibration of even her name tickled Jimmy's awareness, and his body sometimes shivered in delight. "Jenny, I think that life is pushing us forward in the same way that it nudged us together in the first place."

"You think the universe has a plan? That's a big stretch, Jimmy!"

"I know. You're right. It's probably just my mind - whatever THAT is - desiring to be special and believing that the universe has even noticed that it is alive."

"Very egoic. But ego's all we've got, isn't it? This idea that we are separate selves?"

"A rose by any other name... my Jenny!" He blew her a kiss and imagined it crossing the space between them. She pretended that the kiss had found her cheek and tossed her head with the imagined impact. "You really DO love me, Jimmy!"

Their laughter sparkled in the space.

"If the universe had a mind of its own, then we probably haven't decided anything, have we, Jenny?"

"I think it all unfolds just the way it is meant to, Jimmy, but I have no idea where the pattern arises. You know, the 'Divine plan.'"

"Mind wants to believe in one, doesn't it, Girlfriend? But what if there is no plan at all, and we are tumbling through space like dice on a craps table, waiting to see our numbers come up?"

"Well, we'd be winners the entire time that the dice were rolling, Jimmy!"

"That could be a lifetime, Baby!" And he laughed, looking to her for acknowledgment. She mirrored his laugh, and he loved her more for that.

"Let's go to Vegas!" They said it together and then said "freeze" at the same time, pointing fingers and laughing loudly.

"There is only dreaming."

168 JJ'S TUMBLE

"Once, there was doubt.
Now, life's a walkabout!"

Jimmy used to "Measure twice, cut once." That was before he developed his sixth sense to the point he could "Look once, see it done." This practice helped a lot, the steps in between rolling out like a movie, written in awareness as if it always existed, waiting to be perceived.

Then, Jenny.

At first, Jimmy hadn't "seen" it. The "future JJ" didn't exist. Jimmy was careful and measured. His world was shifting step by step, and he was dragging his feet. Then, "quantum entanglement." Jimmy's world shifted as if connected to some distant future he had been previously unaware even existed. Gestalt theory became the ruling factor until experience reached the 100th monkey, and the "shift hit the fan."

"I'm All In," Jimmy said. And he was.

Jimmy's mind was in it "up to his eyeballs," and all he could see was every streaming moment with Jenny, reaching back into the past. The feelings of love were born in time and place, in many faces; looking forward, Jimmy could "feel the earth move under his feet." He had jumped off the cliff of love, and all he could do now was to fly.

"Jenny!" Jimmy called out her name from the kitchen. He was certain that he had heard her move in the other room, some part of his attention seemingly always aware of her presence now. "Are you ready for coffee?"

Jenny didn't have to think about it long. The light was already peeking around the blinds at the window, and her body wanted to start moving again - she knew it was time to begin another day, and she was immediately excited to be doing it with Jimmy again.

"I'm in," she called out to him.
And she was.

*"I feel the sky tumbling down
whenever you're around."
~ Carole King (and JJ)*

169 JJ'S MOMENT

"Remembering is living, past to present.
There's nothing to lose.
Love never forgets."

In the streaming sense of Now, Jimmy could see that this present moment carried every note and lyric that he had ever heard, playing such a symphony in his heart and mind that he might forget the passage of Time.

There was always the story; he never tried to deny that, but he simply wanted something more and found it by wanting less.

"Less is more at the thinking store."

'I wonder,' he thought, 'of all the things I'm not, this moment's what I've got, and that seems to be a lot.' Jimmy's mind often found life poetic now that love became his medic.

'Again,' (he thought) 'I wake to love the same! I thought life was like a cruel game, having loved and lost and loved again; why couldn't love remain? And now, I feel twice as good, knowing love just as I could, feeling as I hoped I would, like everything's new in the world.'

Jenny.

Now, she symbolized love in all its guises: friend, lover, sympathizer, partner, dancer, "realizer." Life was just a "funner" place with Jenny's love and Jenny's face.

"Jenny," he said, his voice resonating with the love that he always felt now that she had become so integral to him. "Jenny, I think that you and I have found what everyone is looking for!"

"I see the excitement in your eyes, Jimmy! Just what ARE you thinking?"

"Well, that's just it! I'm thinking less and loving more, and it has opened up my heart's door! When I look around and stare, I can see Love everywhere! Even if it wasn't there before, I can feel it even more!"

"When I look at your bright smile," he turned to her, held thought a while, "it thrills me, knowing you're 'with me,' and together we shall travel!"

"I'm ready, Jimmy! Let's go!"

"That's just what I'm talking about, Girlfriend! I say, 'wanna?' And you say, 'I'm gonna!' No wonder I'm a goner!"

"Man overboard!"

"That's the truth!"

"Life is a journey
of shared moments."

170 JJ'S LIGHT

"Someone told me it's all happening at the zoo..."
~ Paul Simon

Jimmy had seen so many people in all of his travels. Some he recognized by sight, others he recognized by character, and so many more he didn't know at all (and didn't care if he ever did!)

'Everyone is different and the same,' he thought, 'a rose by any other name...' Jimmy left the thought unfinished. He'd promised himself to judge less and listen more, except at restaurants, when people talked loud enough for anyone to judge. 'So many different looks,' Jimmy mumbled in his mind, 'so many kinds.'

Jenny was not only his Muse but also a sort of "conscience," mirroring him when he was too judgmental, reminding him to soften the eyes that looked upon the world, that "everyone sees things differently," not just him. She could repeat his philosophizing back to him, so appropriately tuned to his frequency and mood. Jenny reflected light like a fine diamond, her many facets both dazzling and attracting him.

"Jenny, you are such a gem!" Jimmy lifted his glass of wine to toast her.

"I'm just reflecting your light, Jimmy!" Jenny said it without hesitation or doubt. She clinked her glass on his, "To us!"

"To us," Jimmy concurred and nosed his wine and drank deeply.

"You reflect me so well," he continued as he set his glass back on the table. "But can you tell me what I'm thinking right now?"

"You're thinking this wine is pretty good, but the Oregon wine might have been brighter."

"Touche, Jenny! Touche!" Jimmy lifted his glass again.

Jenny lifted hers and set it back down. "And now you're thinking how much you love me."

"Well, true, but that's like always true!" Jimmy quipped and took another sip. "It IS a nice reflection on you!"

They both laughed, eyes twinkling with images of each other, cherished and sparkling in the light of the setting sun.

"All love is light.
All light is love."

171 JJ'S WISH

"Magic happens when you let it."

All Jimmy really knew was that he was happier now than before as if a door had opened to let in more light.

The light was Jenny.

Jimmy had dreams, Jenny had dreams, and the more they dreamed together, the better the dream seemed!

Sometimes, Jimmy could only look at her with amazed eyes, allowing thought to cease (or at least idle) and drink in the moment of knowing, knowing that she wanted to be with him, talk with him, play with him, stay with him. Sometimes, it took his breath away.

Just like the Wizard of Oz Scarecrow, they could "while away the hours, conferrin' with the flowers, consultin' with the rain..." Even the simplest things brought joy! So, they did a lot of simple things together, hand in hand, playing in the sand. And life was good.

Then, dreams really did come true! Not that they had any "power" to push their life together in any certain direction, but more like the synchronicity of saying one thing or another and things appearing as if the universe were listening in and arranging things to suit. Isn't that how dreams work? It's certainly how love works.

"Jenny." He said it softly as he studied her face while she silently drifted. In his mind, the sound of her name, even spoken softly, would draw her awareness to the moment that he was "in." There was a pause while time and the universe did their magic, and then her eyes blinked open.

"Jimmy. Are you awake?"

"Yup. And so are you, now!" He grinned.

Jenny wasn't immediately grinning, so Jimmy ventured another word or two: "I love you, Jenny!"

"I love you, too, Boyfriend. But isn't it early?"

"Just the time change, Darling. It's already seven o'clock! And... wait for it... we're still in Vegas!"

"No way!"

"Way! You dreamed it this way! 'No more winters,' you said. I think the Universe heard you."

"Well, that IS a good thing!" Jenny sat up. "We're going to stay here?"

"Yup. Pretty soon, It's June!"

"We're going to the moon!"

"Sort of, but not quite! It's a lot warmer here."

"Then, I'm in!"

"Yup! Me, too! Let's go get sunburnt!"

"But what will I wear?"

"Less is more in Vegas, Darling."

"Ha! I know what you're doing!"

"Just loving you, Baby!"

"You dreamed it this way."

"We did, didn't we."

"Allowing is just
waking up in a different place
and being okay with that."

172 JJ'S TALE

"The Universe turns on our stories."

Whenever Jimmy stopped to "look back," he noticed that his "Now" had a lot of his "Then" included in it, as if there really had been a progression of some sort, and this amazing dream that he was living was composed of all the dreams he had ever had! Unfortunately, some of his past traits that he didn't like also followed him into his present - frustration when things didn't go right, flow right, or know right. Jimmy had developed a great philosophy of "going with the flow," but he wanted to control the flow! He also knew that effort required energy expense, and he wanted this to be efficient - very efficient - perfectly efficient. These principles struggled with each other a bit.

Thinking didn't help, although "intention" seemed to be composed of it, and he enjoyed having his "best of intentions" fulfilled.

Thank god that love only asked him to "allow" - allow that he was worthy to be loved, allow that he could love in return, allow that love was all that truly mattered.

Love was his "way out" of all frustration, inducing him to "look on the world with soft eyes" that required no certain outcome or perfection. "Loving What Is" aligned with "Go With The Flow" being the "Best of Intentions."

And there Jimmy lived - in the balance of mind and heart, thoughts and love, perception and reception, and inception. And, he supposed, there might not be anywhere else to live as a human.

"Jenny." Jimmy knew that Jenny was a miracle in his life. Her love had pulled him out of thought and into feeling, the seeming culmination of every idea of Love that he had ever held, and he looked at her with soft eyes. "Jenny, I'm so glad you showed up in my life!"

"That goes for me, too, Jimmy."

"Now, that sharing love is the "Number 1" thing that I want to do, everything else matters less."

"Everything else is just context, right?"

"You got it! That's another thing I love about you - not only do you 'get' me, but you remind me of my own best thoughts!"

"You're easy to read, my darling. And easy to love!"

"Awwww. See what I mean!" He leaned in to kiss her. "You're my perfect partner!"

"JJ's World thrives, Jimmy!"

"Yes, it does. And we thrive in it."

"Even JJ's World is just a concept, you know. One that we've chosen as a backdrop in which to love more."

"It's a good world, Jenny. I guess we dreamed that people would notice how well we love..." Jimmy's voice trailed off as he considered images of them together, dancing, eating, and playing together.

"We DO love well, Jimmy. And that's all we need."

"That's part of the dream, too, isn't it, Jenny? That we love like a fairy tale and live like one."

"It's a good story, Jimmy, and a good way to live."

"And the Universe seems to reflect our joy. I just have to keep 're-minding' myself so that thinking doesn't push loving out of the way."

"Love does tend to 'step aside' to that 'thinking man.' He can be a bit of a bully, you know."

"That's the one thing I want to remember - not to think too much. It can get in the way of joy."

"You always come around again, Boyfriend."

Jimmy turned to her, smiling. "Is it any wonder?" He kissed her again, slowly this time, cherishing the moment that their lips touched, relishing the joy of sharing touch and intimacy, breathing deeply of the love they shared.

"Now that, that was a kiss!" Jimmy joked, breaking away from the moment, interjecting a phrase from their early courtship.

"Yes. Yes, it was. And yes, it is!" Jenny looked at him, grinning. And they lived happily ever after.

"Love clears out
all the mental debris
of every previous story
we carry around with us.
If we allow it."

173 JJ'S LINE

"Love is a mirror."

Jimmy had looked for love all his life, just like everybody else. He had always thought of himself as "different," but lately, he was beginning to see that Who he thought of as "me" was really everyone that he could see, perception being "one" with the perceiver.

Although he had circled this truth in many books and "talking stick circles," it was when he fell into love that the truth poured into him as if he were a hollow mold, waiting on some liquid ore.

He had written a line in a book, once, and not clearly understood what his mind was telling him, then: "... making love to himself in the shadow of the world." Now, he realized that "he" was part of the shadow, too, and "Love Is All There Is."

Loving truly meant letting go of the sense of "Self," no longer separate from anyone or anything. It was all one fantastic dream! And "he" was free to live it however he wanted it, beginning with right where he believed he had been and where he was going.

Transitions.

Jenny.

Love.

Love was his new pathfinder, and Jenny pointed to the path. All the rest was context, transitioning from one storyline to the next smoothly so as not to totally upset the dream of a nervous system or the ideas of time and continuity.

Love was the new "constant," and Jenny was, too. The rest was "energy squared" or some other nonsensical equation of the mind.

"Jenny." Jimmy noticed how her name bubbled up into his awareness whenever his thoughts turned to love (which was often). "Jenny, I am amazed, still, at this crazy love we found together. Are we making it all up?"

"Jimmy!" Jenny's voice sparkled with his name as if he were the answer to all of her previous questions in life. "Of course, we are making it all up. That's what we 'DO,' remember?"

"Oh, yeah. 'The human condition,' thing, again. Experience is the story that we dream about what is going on. I don't know why I keep forgetting that."

"Don't worry, Boyfriend. I'll keep 're-minding' you. It's what I DO!" Her voice tinkled with laughter.

"It Is What It Is, isn't it?" He joined in her laughter.

"What else could it be?" Jenny giggled out.

"Me?"

"You know there is no 'You' without 'Me,' Jimmy."

"Back to that, are 'We,' Jenny?" He emphasized the "We."

It seemed that they had each dreamed separately of such a laughing, loving, listening partnership of love, but in the "Here Now" of it, in the "Living Out" of it, it seemed as if they truly shared the same dream, only they dreamed it as "One." And they definitely were making it up as they went along!

Jimmy could feel it unfold in every kiss that stopped the mind's spinning and sent the senses reeling, just like he had always dreamed, only better.

Jenny could sense it in every part of her: her body that looked for his touch; her mind that yearned for him to keep talking; her spirit that lived in heightened expectation and joyful experience. He was the "One." She knew that and built upon it.

"Jenny," Jimmy spoke into the silence between thoughts. "Let's keep doing this, 'K?"

"Yes," she broke from her reverie to "join" her awareness with his. (As if there were "two.")

"Where do we want to go today?"

"Anywhere, so long as we do it together!"

"Love in every moment,
and both Love and the Moment
will endure."

174 JJ'S SHARE

"Being comfortable is a state of mind.
Growth is a state of the heart."

Jimmy had always liked his "comfort zone." It wasn't that he didn't try new things - because he did, and he had gotten used to the changes that brought - it was just easier for him when he knew what to expect, and his mind was always busy with those expectations. Jimmy knew that life wasn't linear, though, and so he kept a little "fail-safe" doubt at hand to temper his hopes and dreams.

"I knew it" was one of his favorite remarks when things went wrong. It seemed that Jimmy knew a lot.

Until love showed up again.

He had to admit that he had held onto doubt for as long as he could, tempering his expectations of happiness. But the house of cards came tumbling down when love blew a little breath sideways, gently nudging him from his comfort zone of skepticism and disbelief.

Jenny brought something new to the table, and he wasn't ready for it.

"Jenny." Jimmy knew that this amazing new appearance of love in his life had inexplicably connected him to this woman. She had become a part of him, and now there was no parting. "Jenny, I never used to believe in 'Fate,' like our lives were predestined or something.

But it does seem that we were meant to be together."

"Because we fit together so well, Jimmy?"

"That's definitely true! But I think it's even more than that. It's as if the Universe wanted to use us to show everyone how good love can be and how it can happen even if you're not the same size!" Jimmy laughed and tickled her ribs.

"But we ARE the same size in our magic bed, Jimmy!"

"That's true, too!" He laughed with her. "But there IS the 'standing up' part, after."

"Obviously, you wanted me to be short - a 'diminutive woman,' as your story goes, remember?" Jenny poked fun at him with his own story of being reincarnated as a large man because he was a "diminutive woman" in a previous lifetime, and in this life, he was to "protect and serve" diminutive women.

"More 'Fate,' see? Is it true, or does the mind like making things up to seem true?"

"That would be hard to tell the difference, Jimmy. Wouldn't it?"

"I suppose so, Jenny girl. You seem to have many of the best attributes of all of my previous 'loves' rolled into one tidy package. Maybe that's because the mind couldn't manage much more, and 'fate' is just a mental resolution of what is happening anyway."

"I think I see what you mean, Jimmy. But I'm not any of your 'past loves.' I'm me. And you love me as much as I love me." Jenny grinned. "I mean as much as I love you!"

"I think you had it right the first time, Girlfriend."

"What you see is what you get?"

"Yup. You know it."

"And so do you, Boyfriend."

"Sharing dreams
inevitably
leads to Love."

175 JJ'S STORM

"Thunderstorms can make us small,
remembering Nature's ten miles tall."

Jimmy had always liked thunderstorms. When everyone else ran inside to watch the lightning from behind windows, feeling the thunder rattle the glass, Jimmy was out in it, arms raised to the sky, breathing the ozone, vibrating with the power in the dark air. He knew this was his true nature - soul as black as all the night, with stars and moon in view, and lightning flashes, thunder, too. He never thought that he might be killed by lightning, only that he was thrilled by it, and probably born from it.

Jimmy remembered that as a kid, a neighbor boy had been hit by lightning and lived. Jimmy wondered if he had lived differently after that...

Jenny changed everything.

The dark in Jimmy dispersed, replaced by the light of a new sun, Love shining so bright, he could see nothing else. Jimmy laughed at the thought of counting and dividing by five to see how far away love really was - it was immediate, and he had been struck repeatedly until it thundered in him, becoming the height and depth of him, the very life and breath of him. Love was the ever-present storm, raining joy and watering the fields with peace.

"Jenny." Like the word "thunderstorm," the name of Jenny carried with it all the power and impact of past remembrances of love and all the present pleasure of presence and prescience. "Jenny, I love a good storm, don't you?"

They had been watching the lightning flashes break the night and marveling at the thunder that could shake a house.

"It's the magnificence of nature," Jenny responded.

"It makes me feel small from here. Wanna run out in it?"

"Jimmy, it doesn't surprise me a bit that you would want to run out in it when everyone else is running inside."

"I've always loved the power of it and the raining down of it like energy recharging the earth."

"I think you get recharged by it, too, Boyfriend."

"That's just it, exactly!" Jimmy exclaimed. "I used to run wild in a good summer storm and felt like I was a part of it!"

"Again, no surprise at all."

"I'm content to lie here with you, holding you. I can still feel the connection to the world through you!"

"Love is All There Is, Jimmy. That's what you say!"

"And it's so true. We just forget. I forgot. I still forget from time to time, but you're here to remind me."

"I like that thought, Jimmy." Jenny snuggled in tighter to his big, warm body. "I want to spend as much time here as possible, reminding you to love."

"I'm definitely 'in' for that, Girlfriend!" Jimmy turned to wrap his arms tightly around her, to feel the shock of her closeness, to know the lightning that flashed in him as life charged itself with the energy of love.

"Don't fear the storm.
Embrace it."

176 JJ'S KITE

"Fairy tales really do come true."

**"Pausing is the best way to see something
you might otherwise have missed."**

Flow. For Jimmy, it was always about the flow. The flow of traffic, the flow of information, the flow of communication - flow described how Jimmy related to everything that seemed to arise in the flow of perception - as if it were all his own streaming channel.

And it was.

If Jimmy wanted to be happy, he just had to choose it. If he thought he needed to work a little harder (for whatever reason), inevitably, life would bring something up to shovel. The flow seemed to be a river of reflection, mirroring his ideas of the world, always making him "right" about the way the world worked. The trick was to get ahead of the curve to see that the journey was never done, so he might as well have fun paddling.

And he did.

Jenny seemed to boat the same river. The ripples of her oars on the water crossed and blended with Jimmy's, creating a pattern that looked and sounded like music.

It was.

"Jenny," Jimmy began, noticing how thoughts of her colored

everything. "Jenny, life just seems 'funnerer' with you."

"For me, too, Boyfriend! I hope this shared dream never ends!"

"Eventually, we may just explode if the 'happiness level' gets any higher."

"The air does seem thinner up here!"

"It's 'rare air,' Jenny. 'JJ's World' seems to flow on its own, 'far from the madding crowd.'"

"Let's go fly a kite, Jimmy!"

"Literally or figuratively?"

"It's a metaphor."

"Well then, sure! And may our tails stay aligned!"

> *"Life can be steered*
> *even if it's not going anywhere..."*

177 JJ'S CHOICE

"Mind can let us down,
but Love is steady at the helm."

"If you want to be happy in the dream, just choose it." Jimmy had heard and read this again and again and made the choice again and again, and still, his mind could wander off course. Thank god his heart was leading!

Jimmy had never felt love like this before, and he sure wasn't choosing anything that changed that unless it made love deeper. Jenny really was his mirror - if he could see joy beaming from her face, then he knew everything was in the right place.

"Jenny," he said, his heart and mind aligned, "are we awake?"

"You are, Jimmy. Now let me sleep."

"I won't bug you long, Darling. I just wanted to tell you how much I love you."

"I never get tired of hearing that, you know."

"I never get tired of saying it!"

"Two birds with one word! Well, okay, one phrase."

"Very efficient, don't you think?"

"It doesn't get much better than that, Boyfriend."

"Let's keep it that way."

"That's my agenda, Batman!"

"Holy burritos, Batgirl!"

"That too!"

"Freeze!"

"To join minds,
first, join hearts."

178 JJ'S RIGHT

"If loving you is wrong,
I don't want to be right."

Jimmy, or the entity that called itself "Jimmy," always wanted to be right. Of course, the "right way" was always the way that this "Jimmy" saw it. "Jimmy" had learned to live alone for most of his life. The two thoughts might not be related, but they probably were, even in "Jimmy's" mind. He could, therefore, pronounce judgment on himself and know that he was "right" about that, too. The consequences varied.

"Jimmy" enjoyed "doing" things. This gave him a chance to show how things could and should be done, greatly improving "Jimmy's" opinion of himself. "Jimmy" was disappointed when things didn't work out, having developed a knack for believing that they would. This belief system also served "Jimmy," as you might imagine, even the "wrong" results serving to affirm that there was a "Jimmy" to discern the difference.

And then, "Jenny."

"Jenny" remained a mystery to "Jimmy," even if he did know (mostly) what pleased her and what upset her. "Jenny" remained the miracle that she was, appearing from nowhere to see enough "good" in "Jimmy" to allow his judgment of himself to fade, at least a little. He found that he really was worthy to love and be loved in return, as impossible as that had seemed in his solitary judgment.
Everything changed after that.

"Flow" was still an overriding factor in "Jimmy's" world, and the parts that had "Jenny" in them seemed to flow well, being based on love, as even "Jimmy" knew it. He was becoming accustomed to it, and he didn't want his many failures to affect the level of joy that he was experiencing in this new place of "non-judgment." But the Flow seemed to be calling "Jimmy" to do more and more in less time than ever before, and he was getting tired. And even in the "Mind of Jimmy," there were limits to his abilities to "git 'er done." "Jimmy" planned his time well, so any mistakes were not due to mismanagement, so lack of completion meant there was a lack in "Jimmy." Heaven forbid.

"Jenny." "Jimmy" always thought of her as a miracle in his life and tried to always hold her in the light of perfection. "Jenny, I have no idea what you see in me. Maybe deep down, some prehistoric sense of survival says that I might be 'strong enough' and 'smart enough' to take care of you, even if you don't need to be 'taken care of.'"

"Jimmy," you are such a nerd and a nut! Did you ever think that you think too much?"

"Well, naturally, I've thought that. Typically, I'd have to dismiss the idea, though, as it is a bit 'self' destructive."

"Hmm. I thought you were trying to get out of that 'self' a bit. Or did I get that wrong?"

"You're right, 'Jenny.' You're always right. And that's a great reflection on 'me!'"

"But, Jimmy, we all mess up once in a while. We all need a little 'forgive and forget.' I've heard you say that yourself."

"Thanks for reminding me. I can be a bit hard on myself, too. That 'self-judgment' thing, you know."

"Well, we're both better together than we were apart."

"The whole is greater than the sum of its parts?"

"You, me, and Aristotle think so." Jenny laughed in the way that she did, which made everything seem hilarious.

"That makes Two of Us... or maybe three!" Jimmy laughed with her, enjoying the release of it. Laughter always seemed to be like a "reset" button for "Jimmy."

"Thanks, Jenny, for straightening 'me' out now and then. It's a 'mon-u-mental' task. You see what I did there?"

"I see you, 'Jimmy,' clear and bright. Did you know that thinking never got anything done?"

"Only 'doing?'"

"'Being' is more like it, Boyfriend."

"Let it 'Be?'"

"You, me, and Jude this time!"

"A likely story."

"Sing it with me?"

"I just wanna hold your hand, Jenny."

"That, too. Just let me into your heart..." "Jenny" started singing the Beatles lyrics, and "Jimmy" joined her.

"Then we can start to make it better."

"The moment you let her under your skin,
then 'You' begins..."
~ The Beatles (and JJ)

179 JJ'S BLISS

"On a good day,
they could see forever..."

Jimmy and Jenny were joined at the dreams. Life as they now knew it was more than each of their pasts - a dream they might have read about, a fairy tale that no one believed could really come true. Yet, here they were, living life as they had only dreamed before, and knowing that there was more past each door, they no longer kept score.

"So much to explore!" They both said, laughing and shaking their heads.

"Jimmy." Jenny always said his name with a lilt as if drawing his attention gave her a shot of energy. "Jimmy, are we really going to love forever?"

"Jenny! You know it," he said, turning toward her for a hug and a kiss. "What do you see when you close your eyes and look at the future?"

"I see lots more of this!" Jenny responded gleefully.

"And so, it shall be!" Jimmy joined her, laughing.

Every morning, as consciousness reopened their eyes to the world, Jenny and Jimmy dawdled in bed, enjoying each other's presence, sharing the joy that each found waking up together again and relishing the love that still glowed in their hearths. And the fire of the day returned with the dawn.

"Jenny." Jimmy could feel the love that he had attached to her name call forth those same feelings that he had been imprinted with when they first said, "I'm in." "Jenny, I can't wait to explore more life with you!"

"Is it 'Live,' or is it Memorex?" Jenny quoted the old TV commercial for cassette tapes.

"It's very 'Live,' Girlfriend. No rehearsals needed."

"Or wanted, Boyfriend! I love being 'open' to what life brings to us!"

"It's the only way to travel!"

"The journey is best measured in friends, Darling, and you're my Bestie."

"Life is short, and the world is wide, Little One! Let's have fun together!"

"You can call me Darlin', Darlin'!"

"Just don't call you late for lovin'!"

They paused the world with a hug and a kiss, enjoying the bliss of joined intention and shared dreams. The world was made of love, it seemed, and might not ever end.

"Not all those who wander are lost."
~ Gandalf (J.R.R. Tolkien)

180 JJ'S FILTER

"In the big scheme,
there are only dreams..."

Synchronicity and Serendipity. Jimmy had always loved these words, the ideas behind the concepts, the movies and philosophies that were based on them, and, most of all, finding them in his own life! It made life seem more magical to see it as part of some heavenly scheme as if there were order in his dreams and meaning in life's memes. 'Why not enjoy the ride,' he thought, smiling a lot.

When Jimmy and Jenny danced, they sometimes wondered if they were dancing to the music or if the music was arising from the joy of their dancing! Often, people commented on the joyful play of their movements. Jimmy and Jenny had always been amazed at how well they fit together: they danced alike, ate alike, enjoyed the same music, laughed at the same jokes, even thinking alike! Now that they had lived together for several years, they enjoyed the nuances - the small differences that made each unique, and they celebrated the big ones, like Jimmy being a man and Jenny being a woman. Life was good together, and they knew it.

"Jenny." Jimmy spoke her name as if calling a new world into existence, "Before Jenny," giving way to "Now Jenny."
"Jenny, isn't it amazing how everything has worked out? It's not perfect, except that it is no matter what, but I sure wouldn't have it any other way!"
"Jimmy, life is amazing with you! I wouldn't have it any other way,

either! It's an adventure!"

"We do stay busy, don't we?"

"But we take time to recover, too."

"That's a good thing, Jenny! A little sleep never hurt anyone!"

"Said the guy who sleeps just enough to make his hair look funny in the morning."

"Well, it IS a look, Dear One. Albeit not a great one!" They laughed together, enjoying the banter.

"Do you hear the birds chirping, Jenny? I think they do that just for us."

"Well, for you, you mean. You're the one up at the crack of dawn!"

"But if I'm happy, you're happy, right? So, they really do it for both of us!"

"So, no matter what happens good to either of us, it's good for both of us, Jimmy?"

"Exactly! The more, the merrier!"

"I'm not sure that's what that originally meant, Jimmy..." Her voice trailed off with a grin.

"It's just like the song lyrics that we change to fit the moment, Jenny. It's all for us, you know."

"ALL of It?"

"It's all so synchronous. When we're happy, the world seems happier, don't you think?"

"That's it for sure, Jimmy."

"Good fortune happens for those who notice it!"

"See it to believe it. And vice versa!"

"I see you, Jenny!"

"Avatar was for us, too, wasn't it...?"

"As a matter of course."

They gazed into each other's eyes, mesmerized by the light of the stars there.

"It's All for you!"

181 JJ'S GIFT

"Intimacy is growing together,
sharing one heart.
Sharing showers is also part!"

Jimmy had lived alone for many years before Jenny moved in. He had gotten used to watching certain TV shows and eating familiar foods for dinner, going to bed when he wanted, and getting up early to write.

None of this changed when Jenny moved in. It just got better! "Everything's better, shared," Jenny said, and Jimmy believed it. He shared everything! And that became the linchpin of their relationship - they both held nothing back, revealing their secrets from past lives and letting each other see the troublesome zits of the "Now." Whatever each feared, they shared. Whenever each hurt, they cared. Together, they dared to try new things and go to new places that they would've skipped alone. Together, they made a home wherever they roamed. The feeling of freedom that came with this openness kept a smile on their faces for each other and for all the unsuspecting people who showed up in their lives.

Living together and loving each other was a day-to-day thing. Every morning, waking up to share the gift of another day, they grinned broadly at each other, acknowledging how fine it was to share time on the planet holding hands and holding each other close.

Every night, they sat up close together in bed and talked about the day before they slid down, touching as much skin as possible, then

184

drifting off to Neverland.

The days were filled with "regular stuff" that was somehow more special when they did it together. Holding hands felt more natural than walking alone. Whether they were mowing the lawn or solving a crossword puzzle, they looked at each other and smiled, happy to be in each other's company. They chose to be happy every day.

"Jenny." Jimmy felt the taste of her name on his tongue like the sweetness of chocolate. "Jenny, I'm still amazed that out of all the billions of people on the planet..." He paused for effect and to let her attention come a bit closer, then he continued, "... I'm sure glad you don't speak Chinese!" They had both expected him to say, "I'm so glad we found each other," so they both laughed at the incongruity, which also spoke of the truth - that they were so suited for each other that they held a winning hand.

"And I'm glad that you know a little French!" Jenny quipped as she rolled her eyes and waggled her tongue at him.

"Me, too!" Jimmy declared truthfully.

"Who knew 'multilingual' could be so fun!"

"You are such a nut!" Jenny shook her head. "And that's part of what I love about you."

"Ditto, Darling. Lily Darling." Jimmy used the nickname that he had created for her by slurring "Little Darling One." The name came to represent the "new" person she was becoming as she grew closer to him. "Big Daddy Jim" was his pseudonym, describing his variance in height and breadth. They had become new creatures in this state of love that they shared.

"Jenny, I really am glad - and sometimes still amazed - that you are still here with me! How did I get so lucky?"

"I'm not sure how it happened, but you're right - you're a lucky man!" She grinned, knowing the Truth of it and knowing how it applied to her side of things. "And I'm the luckiest girl on the planet."

Jimmy swooped to kiss her, and they broke apart, laughing. "It's a great dream we've made here." Jimmy continued. "And it seems so real!" He pinched her as if to check her "realness." She slapped at his hand, scolding him. "It's real, all right! Now be gentle with the girl."

"Can I tickle?"

"Gently, Boy."

Jimmy grinned at her, with the look of a foolish young boy in love for the first time. Jenny laughed and pointed at his face. "That look! Like you could eat me up!"

"Well, I could, you know. You ARE pretty tasty!" He slurped his tongue.

"Yikes! Time out!" She backed away, laughing and protesting.

"Whenever you're ready, Girlfriend, I'm right here."

"How about a rain check while you get us both coffees?"

"I'll be baa-ack," Jimmy called to her as he slid from the bed and headed to the kitchen.

"I'll be here waiting for you!" And she would be, and he would be.

And the dream would go on.

**"Time together
is the greatest gift."**

182 JJ'S WONDER

"Wonder where I go in dreams?
Wonder IS where I go in dreams."

Jimmy wondered about things: which is real, and which is the illusion being one of the most prevalent. The problem that he had was that there was no way to prove anything was real if it all arose from perception, and perception was totally subjective. Ultimately, it always came to this - that his perception, governed as it was by long-held belief systems (whether right or wrong) and filtered by his programmed responses and understanding, was still all that he had to go on and all that he ever would have. Period. If the table kept his cup in suspension, it seemed real enough. His cup had never fallen through - he was certain of that. Scientists (who were those guys?) had determined that everything was made of atoms and that atoms were mostly space.

This applied to the cup, too, and the coffee in it, and the hand that put it there. His hand put it there. His hand was motivated by his mind - which he knew was mostly a collection of distorted ideas about the world of experience - so everything arose from the Mind.

Jimmy was right back where he started.

Jimmy started at the edge of perception, where the light sometimes flickered. Or was that a trick of the eyes? In a sense, everything was made of light. He could only see things because of light reflection and refraction, and even then, didn't the Mind have to turn the image upside-down or something? Jimmy found it interesting that his nearsightedness was getting better as he grew older. But were things any clearer? And who was doing the seeing, anyway? It was all so wonderful and inexplicable. And that was as real as it gets.

Jenny was a persistent part of his waking dream now, and Jimmy didn't want it any other way. She was cute, she was fun, she was smart, witty, and generally happy, and (it seemed to Jimmy) genuinely happy to see him, too! If their dreams had somehow connected and merged, that was also amazing and perfect! If there were a Director of things perceived, Jimmy was good with the plot and the mystery and the sex scenes. The writing seemed superlative! This was one catnip ride that Jimmy didn't ever want to get off of!

"Jenny," Jimmy always felt a little giddy when he acknowledged that she was present, "Do you think that we'll ever know what's really going on here?"

"Jimmy, you're doing it again." Jenny loved the boy in him who wondered and wrote and wore strange clothes. "You're thinking too much."

"But you said you liked it when I described my belief systems and my stories of how they worked or didn't and how they changed along the way."

"Yup, I still do, Boyfriend."

"Well, they are still changing, so I have to think about what's going on a little to sort it out, you know."

"Sounds exhausting!" Jenny commiserated.

"It can be if I dream it that way. Or it can be energizing and freeing if I believe it that way!"

"I'm a believer." Jenny loved the interplay, Jimmy's lead, and her "follow." Jimmy was also good about letting her lead by choosing, too. "Couldn't leave yer if I tried." She mangled the old Monkees lyric.

"Ba dum pum." Jimmy pretended to play a drum flourish. "Not a trace of doubt in my mind... And that's exactly what I love about you!"

"My ability to misremember lyrics?" Jenny quipped.

"That, for sure! And that you play with the thoughts running through your mind... just like me. Maybe I made you up?"

"Well, if you did make me up, you sure did good!"

"That's for sure!" They both laughed and kissed at the end.

"I guess all we can do is 'go with the flow,' right, Girlfriend?"

"Sounds good to me."

"I thought it would..."

"Isn't that a bit self-fulfilling?"

"Everyone is their own best prophet."

"You should put that on a t-shirt!"

"I did. I keep it in the closet with the 'old news.' Nowadays, it's all about Present Moment Awareness."

"That doesn't fit on a t-shirt, I don't think."

"Exactly. Now, get over here and hug me."

"As you wish..." She said, grinning. "Especially when I wish it, too."

"It's All good."

"Life is a fairy tale.
Make it a good one,
with a happy ending."

183 JJ'S RASTA

"Holding to this point of view:
Nothing's better than Love with you."

Jimmy had "been around the block" a few times and certainly didn't need to know anything different, having figured it all out long ago. Or so he thought.

Then, Jenny.

Confused by the unexpected appearance of love again, Jimmy at first retreated to his cave of beliefs, thinking contentment lived there. But, once aroused, love could not be contained or lessened or hidden, and Jimmy peeked out and was immediately tagged. "You're It!" And he was.

"Jenny," he sighed her name, knowing that she had become his one joy in life. "Jenny, thank you for hanging out with me and putting up with my idiosyncrasies."
"You're welcome, Jimmy. And I love all of your 'idiot-synchronicities,' you know."
"Hey! That's not what I said!"
"But it's true, and you know it!"
"I can't deny it. I like to believe in magic."
"Pull a rabbit out of your hat?"
"No, but hold my beer and watch this!"

They laughed, bobbling their heads and laughing at that, too. They both knew that words were just to play with, that ideas about the world were mostly gibberish, and that love was best expressed through soft eyes and silent tongues. But the game was "on" again, and they laughed to play in it.

"You're a lot taller in bed, you know."

"You're a lot easier to reach for a kiss in bed, you know." And she leaned over and kissed him, making a shiver run up and down his spine.

"Goddess, I love when you do that!"

"It's your dream, remember?"

"Well, I must've gone 'all out' with this one!"

"Indeed, you did, Boyfriend!"

"In Deed. And in dreams. And, it seems, in reality."

"Oh, this is real," Jenny said slyly, "as real as it gets." And she kissed him again, with the intention to crash his ship on the rocks of her shore.

Jimmy trembled at the pure bliss of her kisses and returned the flavor, focusing every bit of his attention and awareness on the moment. There was nothing but the kiss. His body shook again, love coursing through him like a rampaging river in spring. He blinked his eyes open, still holding her tender yet tightly.

"I do so enjoy our time together." He quipped in a whisper of love.

"It's like there is no time," Jenny responded. "And no world, either."

"Just this."

"Just this," she agreed softly, and she pulled him down again into the abyss.

"There can be only One Love."
~ The Rastafarian Highlander

184 JJ'S BOAT

*"Every windshield
needs washing
once in a while."*

Jimmy had forgotten the thrill of starting over. He had grown comfortable playing in the same space, working at the same place and pace, and generally aligning his tastes and his face with the race. It was all changing again.

Like most changes, this would be for the better, taking him and his Beloved into a new chapter of the story of their lives together. It was the letting go of "what is" without really knowing the "what will be" that was the hardest. The Mind was always more comfortable with what it thought it knew than with what it knew it didn't know. And couldn't know. The "future" was just out of reach, over the cliff, blurry and distant. Jimmy knew they could fly. Jenny knew, too. There was just too much time with the sun on their wings...

Each day leading up to the shift, they realized just how well the Universe had laid Its plans to carry them forward. And now, as they were letting go of more things every day, the itinerary was clear - all the things that were unfolding "here" would draw to a close to take them "there." It was a perfect plan and an easy blueprint to read. If only they could just fall asleep and wake up in their new life without all of this packing and saying goodbye. Yes, the slow transition was making this a gradual letting go to ease the shock, but sometimes, they just wanted to get gone and be done with it. Life was never meant to be lived that way, though. The journey was the journey. Life was always sorting through what was important and to be chosen and kept and what could be let go.

In the end, Love was all that held their full attention, and they turned to it, and Immersed in it.

"Jenny." Jimmy could still feel the twinge of his heart when he spoke her name. "Jenny, the beginning of the end is almost here!"

"How about just the beginning of the everlasting story, Jimmy? I don't think this ever really ends."

"Just a saying, Girlfriend. This Love is too big to ever have an end! But it does feel like the time has become golden, like leaves in the fall."

"You're such a romantic Boyfriend. You have a poet's heart and a philosopher's eye."

"And the brain of a chimpanzee!" Jimmy laughed. Laughing at his shortcomings, he had learned, was the easiest way to keep the mind from dwelling on them.

"There are some similarities... We do like to clean each other!" Jenny was always quick to follow Jimmy into laughter and silliness. Sharing joy is why this worked so well.

"Scrub a dub-dub. Two lovers in a tub!"

"Pat-a-cake, baker's man!"

"Mark you with a 'J?'"

"Too late, Jimmy. I'm a 'marked woman' already!"

"But it's MY magic marker!"

"Oh, yes, it is. Magically delicious."

"Thank you, lucky charms!"

"Will a kiss work?"

"It's the only thing that will!" Jimmy loved the playfulness of this woman. She was right in front of him like a reflection in the mirror. Jenny was how he would be if he were a woman. He was sure of that! He was so glad that she had chosen to join him on this crazy journey. And now they were not only living together but moving together! It felt even bigger if that were possible.

"Jenny, I'm so glad that we found each other."

"Jimmy, it sure is better than anything I'd ever dreamed before."

"Ditto, Baby. And now we're moving to a place of dreams. Are you ready?"

"So long as I'm with you!"

"You can count on that!" He leaned in to kiss her, closing his eyes to all of the rest of the world.

*"Going with the Flow is easy.
Just let go."*

185 JJ'S SEA

*"Every day's
a little different."*

The speed of life seemed to be picking up lately, but Jimmy and Jenny were flowing with it, allowing each day to unfold while aligning their energy and intention with what appeared right in front of them. Like leaves in the river, they moved and spun, watching the surroundings change and things fall away, appearance unnecessary now. They clung to each other, the only living persons in their world.

Jimmy held Jenny's hand and said, "You're mine. You're free as the wind, yet you show up again and again to let me love you. I hope I tell you that enough." He looked at her softly, wrapping his aura around her, caressing her with his attention and intention.

Jenny sighed and returned his loving gaze. There really was no place else that she'd rather be, and she told him that and then added, "Just this, Jimmy. Just this." And she touched her hand to her heart and smiled that smile that all lovers recognize - a pure, simple gaze that wants nothing and gives all.

The Rivers of Time and Space flowed around them in their rock-solid stance of love, and everything floated, the world light as the air, the substance of life that had neither weight nor mass, that flowed unseen everywhere and nowhere at all, existing as if in a dream.

The dream was vital. The dream was everything. It prompted and pulled, teased and cajoled, and each story was told as if true.

"There's nothing you have to do." They'd heard it repeated in books and live streams. They knew it was true, but they had to have dreams. "Nothing is as it seems."

"Jenny." Even the sound of her name held a thrall on him when he spoke it, so deeply ingrained was his desire for her. "Jenny, it's all coming together."

"I love it when we do that, Boyfriend! It's so powerful!"

Jimmy laughed with her, remembering the last ecstatic moment that they shared. "Yes, Girlfriend, you give me the shivers! But isn't it amazing how everything is working out just by following our promptings? I see a bright future ahead..."

"It's amazing, really, Jimmy. It's falling into place like a great game of Tetris!"

"Exciting, isn't it? When everything seems to be sweeping you off your feet to carry you onward." Jimmy made a gesture like someone surfing a great wave, adding a sound effect of wind and landing the rider on a new beach. "And then we're there. Instead of here. It's rather amazing, isn't it." Jimmy stated the last matter-of-factly.

"Let's ride the waves together, Jimmy. That's all I want." Jenny said it softly, almost wistfully, knowing the Truth of it and feeling the love of it in her bones. "Just this."

"Love is the flow of the oceans,
the life of the sea of dreams."

186 JJ'S PRESENT

"The adventure lives in the unknown."

Jimmy had always been fairly confident that he could handle whatever life threw at him. He'd survived this long, hadn't he? And now, he had someone to share in the adventure of stepping into the unknown. They had made practice trips, camping, flying, exploring, and now they moved in synchrony with the flow of life, going "all in" with it, falling into the vast ocean that lay before them, knowing that waves of Love would carry them.

Life was ever imminent, unfolding at the edge of awareness. Jimmy and Jenny looked out from their vantage point onto an unsuspecting world. They saw things as they chose to see them. They most often chose love.

"Jenny, do you see what I see?" Jimmy looked to her for concurrence in the dream, as she represented everything good and loving in his world.

"I see that loving life the way we do together is the best time ever, if that's what you mean, Jimmy." And she meant just what she said.

Jimmy nodded his agreement. "It's as if the Universe is listening and morphing with our desires."

"I see that, too. And all it asks is that we let go and trust."

"We did that with each other, didn't we," Jimmy stated matter-of-factly, turning to look into her eyes for the confirmation that he could always find there.

"Life sings when we sing. 'Nothing but blue skies, do I see!'"

"Nothing but bluebirds, all day long!" Jimmy grinned, modifying the Blue Skies lyrics, "Never saw the sun shining so bright..."

Jenny's eyes were bright and shining, just like the song.

"Nothing but blue skies, from now on..." They sang together, and the world sang along, like the sparrows greeting the dawning sun or the breeze caressing the full moon.

"Life is good, isn't it." Jimmy sighed.

"It's the best it's ever been, Boyfriend."

"With you, silly one!" He tickled her and kissed her nose.

"Playful is as playful does, you know," she responded, poking him in the side.

"Beware the Kraken," Jimmy waved his arms overhead.

"I've got your number, Captain Jack!"

Jimmy collapsed back into the pillows. "Yes, you do, I admit it. All of my power was in my hair." He mussed it up and then pretended to smooth it out.

"And in your sword," she laughed, mussing his hair, too. "But it's Stockholm Syndrome all over again."

"You've fallen for your kidnapper?"

"It seems that way." Jenny feigned remorse. "But at least I'm happy about it!" She brightened and tickled Jimmy's ribs.

"I'm happy, too!" He pretended to battle her. "Now, who's the Kraken!"

"Well, I do like it on top!"

Jimmy mussed her hair, too, then smoothed it behind her ear. "And I'm happy when you're happy!"

"All's well with the world."

"Yes, it is," Jimmy agreed and kissed her deeply, eyes closed to anything but this moment.

"Being present is the present."

187 JJ'S VIBE

"Live in the mystery.
Know only one thing.
The Universe is made of Love."

The Law of Attraction always seemed like such a good answer for the Mind's quest for an answer to how the Universe works. "Are you a vibrational match?" was a good question to ask, whether stuck in the mud or being blown by the whims of time. Jimmy just wasn't sure how to vibrate like something that he had never known before. The Mind was certain it could figure it out. Now, if only Jimmy knew what it was that he really wanted so he could shimmy into it. He fancied himself a good dancer, and that gave him a certain confidence that he could find the right moves and get in the groove of his best intention.

Jimmy thought that alignment and intention were inevitably the same, and the rudder of the ship was his best idea of what life could look like. Naturally, this view changed over time, absorbing new experiences and assimilating the nuggets of truth that the mind could mine. It was all a metaphor anyway, wasn't it? Like some Never-ending Story of life and love, the future kept unfolding into the Now and again, the vast cast of characters playing their parts the best they knew how, and Jimmy playing right along with them.

Then Jenny showed up.

She had entered Jimmy's world almost unseen at first, a ripple on the pond of his mind. Jenny had grown in his awareness, her story slowly resonating with his own, until the vibrational match had overwhelmed them both, sending their dreams tumbling into a future where they were inseparable, though still very distinguishable, except for the silly grins that made their faces, at least, look alike.

The future was very bright, indeed.

Once acknowledged and embraced, Love has no limits except what the Mind is allowed to paint. Jenny and Jimmy knew that "Going all in" required "Letting go" as well. The joy of new love washed away all doubts of what was important, and the world seemed to resonate with this simplistic outlook - that love was all that mattered. Joy to the World - Rinse and Repeat.

And so it was that they found themselves ready and willing to embark on a new journey together into an unknown future, guided by the simplest of intentions: to always move in the direction of Love. Everything else was merely context. That's why the universe could keep utilizing the same characters - only their names had changed to protect their innocence.

"Are you ready, Jenny?"

"Ready is as ready does Boyfriend."

"Then let's go!"

"I'm with you on that!" Jenny said and slid off the edge of the bed and headed for the bathroom.

"That's not the 'go' I was talking about!" Jimmy called to her as she retreated across the hall.

"You'll have to be more specific next time," Jenny called back, laughing.

Once again, they started the day in love and laughing about it, the joy vibrating through both of them and in the air.

*"Laughter
is the shortest way
to Love."*

188 JJ'S SECRET

"The secret to reality is one thing:
Intention, Intention, Intention."

All perception is filtered by the Mind's interpretations of it. No exception. Like the Doobie Brothers lyric, "What a fool believes; he sees..." And there are no "wise men." There is only "Intention" - we project our past before us and walk willingly into it. There is no "coming out" on the other side. There are no doors through, or secret passages, or anything secret at all. It's as plain as the thought on your face. And the thought about your face. And your idea of this place. It's all about Intention, then.

Jimmy knew that how he held an idea in his Mind's eye - be it a person, place, or thing - it was all a part of the dream of consciousness. He couldn't see past it or rise above it, and he didn't want to anymore. The searching for meaning outside himself had dissipated, leaving a clearer understanding that this - whatever "this" is - was "All There Is." And in that singular notion, every moment of life became more intense, and his intention to live it well was now the "One Thing" - that Curly points to in City Slickers - the One Thing that each of us must rediscover on our own.

Jimmy remembered the One Thing some of the time, and other times, it was forgotten in some dusty drawer of the mind. Jenny helped him to remember what he already knew - that Love was part of his own "One Thing" in the dream, or at least pointed towards it. And in that, happiness was Jimmy's to choose, like which pair of shoes or shirt, or Muse to put on. "All in" had saved him, finally, drawing him out of the cave of thought and understanding and into the light of play.

"Jenny." He spoke her name with the familiarity of his own name as if she were a part of him and always had been. "Jenny, I think this is amazing!"

"Which 'this,' Boyfriend? This moment," she paused, "or this one?" She grinned, and Jimmy grinned with her. They seemed to be mirrors of each other.

"Ah, Jenny! That's exactly why I love you!"

"Because I'm here in this moment?" She loved to tease Jimmy about his beliefs.

"Well, yes, that, of course. Or 'this.' Or 'That!'" Jimmy pointed in the air.

"So, the secret to life is 'this or that'? That seems simple enough!" Jenny broke into a giggle.

"Or the other," Jimmy finished the line laughing. "Pick a path and live it up!"

"I like it, Jimmy! Got any more secrets to life you want to share?" She fluttered her eyes at him coquettishly.

"You already know them all, Girlfriend!" He reached to tickle her, and she pretended to fend him off, laughing all the while.

"The secret of life is to follow the tickle?" Jenny spoke rhetorically.

"In a sense. It's not common sense, either. Sixth Sense, maybe."

"You see dead people?"

"They're all around us..." Jimmy spoke furtively, cupping his hand to his brow and peering.

"Let's stay here and stay safe," Jenny whispered. Jimmy whispered back.

"You know that wouldn't work out well at the end of things."

"OK, Gandalf. 'The Journey doesn't end here,' remember?"

"Is this the shore or the sea?" Jimmy inquired.

"Both," answered Jenny, reflecting what they both knew to be true.

*"When you know it's all a dream,
and you choose to be happy anyway,
then you have found the secret to life."*

189 JJ'S TRAIN

*"The surprise
is what's inside!"*

Jimmy had learned the hard way that appearances in the dream were mostly governed by his perception of them. The Mind, with all of its past fears and mistaken realizations, still filtered everything that he saw, colored all that he felt, and ultimately determined the direction of his life. In the Field, where every possibility existed, choosing the "right" way to go would be a simple matter if not for the interference of the Mind and its past frequencies being projected forward into space.

The solution had been a long time coming - pause the Mind to allow some Greater Universal Force to proffer the best path for his spirit to walk.

The Path was Love.

The journey had taken Jimmy from the east to the west, from the north to the south, and a few places in between. Always he had looked for love "in all the wrong places," until he thought that it couldn't be found. And it couldn't. He was right. Only in the state of complete "surrender" to Life could the possibility exist. Jimmy was a bit of a control freak, always wanting to drive everyone's vehicle and correct everyone's grammar - in short, wanting to be "right" about everything he thought he knew. "Giving up" was hard. Jimmy's Mind had a chokehold on his Life.

Then Jenny.

Jenny had come into his life slowly at first and then, with guns blazing, had shot down every defense system that Jimmy's Mind had put in place to guard against an assault on his heart. After a brief struggle, he had raised his heart in surrender and been handed the keys to Paradise.

"Jenny," Jimmy spoke her name almost wistfully at times, knowing that the entire past of his life no longer mattered, gone with the wind of change and the promise to love forever. "Jenny, I can't help thinking..."

"There's your problem right there, Jimmy, in a nutshell." Jenny grinned at him, knowing that she played his Muse and that amused him - and her!

"Yes, of course, that," Jimmy responded, grinning back, "but the Universe does seem to rewrite at least a bit of 'consideration of things,' doesn't it?" He continued. "What I was going to say..."

"Until you were so rudely interrupted?" Jenny quipped.

Jimmy grinned louder. "Yes, that, too. But also... Now I forget what I was going to say!"

"Hmm. Then either it wasn't that important, or it will come around again for you to notice."

"That's it!" Jimmy cried out exultantly. "The Universe seems to work in cycles! Exactly! Like some old locomotive, spinning its wheels as it tries to move its load forward until it grabs enough traction, transfers the energy into momentum, and goes tearing down the tracks toward some future destination!"

"Whew! That's quite an analogy, Boyfriend. And just what fuels this amazing engine of life?"

"I think you already know the answer to that, Girlfriend. You do."

"Little Ol' Me?" Jenny drawled.

"Well, that Love thing that you stirred up. Now I've got bees buzzing, and my head's spinning all the time."

"And your train...?" Jenny questioned him slyly pointing him back to his original premise.

"Oh, it's left the station and is barreling down the tracks towards 'who knows where.' And it's not coming back."

"Love is a powerful thing, Jimmy."

"All the power in the Universe."

"Let's see where this train takes us..."

"My ticket's already punched. I'm in for the long haul."

"Whoo, whoo!" Jenny whistled, pulling an imaginary string to sound the engine. "All aboard!"

*"Allow that the Universe already knows
the best path for your life,
and It will take you there."*

190 JJ'S NOW

"Gonna be hot for a while.
Better wear sunscreen."

Jimmy and Jenny loved the heat. They'd rather eat hot food than cold, choose to drink hot tea or coffee rather than a cola on ice, and prefer sun over snow by a wide margin. Moving south was as natural as the way they had met. Almost predestined.

They had circled the neighborhoods in the area they wanted to live like a dog trying to settle down into his bed. Then, they found the right place and called it home.

Sometimes a place just feels "right." It's almost as if it is familiar, like a déjà vu experience. Maybe the Future really does pull us into it while we stumble along saying, "what happened?" Or "How did we get here?" Eventually, Future settles back into Now, and very little paddling is required to maintain position on the river, like an eddy in Time. It's a lot easier to pause and look around at the beauty of the moment, then.

"Jenny." Although Jenny appeared as a separate individual in the dream, Jimmy sometimes forgot to say her name out loud, whispering to her in his Mind as if she were a part of him and could follow his thoughts. "Jenny, you already know this, but I think we were meant to be here - in this moment."

"Jimmy, of course we are! We're 'here,' aren't we?"

Jimmy liked the saying, "It Is What It Is," and used it often enough. Jenny liked it, too. The acceptance of "what is" meant that the moment could be enjoyed without considering what might be "better" or "worser." Seeing the moment as "perfect" allowed them a brighter experience of it.

"You know it, Girlfriend! This moment is 'home,' and I'm so glad you're in it!"

"Yes. That. Or is it 'This?' I always forget." Jenny loved to play with words and concepts, which encouraged Jimmy to play even more.

"Now is where I want to be." Jimmy sang the words as if they were part of Simon and Garfunkel's "Homeward Bound."

"Now, where my music's playin'..." Jenny picked up the lyric and ran with it. "Now, where my love lies waitin'..."

They finished the lyric together, grinning at each other: "... silently for me."

Jimmy kissed her forehead. "That's what I'm talkin' about!"

"Me, too!"

"What if there really is only 'Us' in this world?"

"Well, Jimmy, there really is 'only Us' in 'JJ's World.'"

"That's sort of true, isn't it? In this moment, where we are exchanging words and feelings and perceptions of all types and sizes..." Jimmy paused to consider the next words, "... We're 'It.' We certainly can't know anything about what someone else is choosing to think, believe, see, or do at this moment. Only what we choose to feel."

"Choose 'happy in the dream,' you always say, Boyfriend!"

"And that's a nice reflection of you!"

They laughed, eyes bright with the knowing that they had chosen each other in the dream and chosen 'happy' right along with it.

"The Prompting is always there
beneath the surface of the moment."

191 JJ'S LOVE

"Love fuels the dream."

In all of his searching, Jimmy had found that all paths lead to one place - the Mind. The Mind looks outside itself into the dream it has projected as if there were something "out there" that didn't have its origins "in here." Perception, brought back to its source, is just that - projection. "See only Love" is more truly stated as "Be only Love." We see what we intend to see all day long. Our "free will" is the ability to choose how we might walk through the dream by tempering our thoughts, watching the mind and its egocentric machinations, and remembering to laugh at all of it!

Laughter, in Jimmy's dream, was one of the most important aspects of love.

Laughter always breaks up the continuity of thought that takes us down the rabbit hole, interrupting the dream to allow Love to be seen by shattering the judgments of ongoing perception.

The Joy of laughter became the ecstasy of love in Jimmy's mind, shaking him and waking him to look within, where the real treasure lay. "Where my Love lies waiting silently for me..."

Jimmy looked at his watch. Then, realizing that it had become a habit to look at what time it was, how fast life was moving, and how much time was left - he slipped it off his wrist like a sprung handcuff and never put it on again. This was years ago now, and life lived in the moment, in the prompting, had become the habit, the pattern, the focal point in the dream. Life swirled around him, pulling his attention towards things he recognized from his past, and he dismissed many, looking from an open heart toward the dream of love and following that path, now so well-lit with his hand and his heart in Jenny's, that they "had to wear shades."

"Jenny!" Jimmy's heart always brightened a bit when he focused his attention on her. "Jenny, I can see our future together, and it feels so bright!"

"That's a great reflection of you, Jimmy! 'Always look on the bright side of life!'" Jenny sang the lyrics from the movie "Life of Brian."

"That really is a great way to look at things, Jenny! I just love how we cast our dreams into the wind and allow our life to be blown sky high!"

"We are having fun, aren't we, Boyfriend." Jenny leaned into him, relishing the closeness, the warmth, the touch, the reality of the man she had grown in Love with.

"Ah, yes, Jenny, we are." Jimmy tried an Irish accent, sounding a little like the leprechaun from Lucky Charms fame. "And what choice did we 'ave, really, when we were filled with such joy whene'er we're together, now, my Dearie?"

"Why, none at all, Captain!"

"As you like it!"

"And ye', too!"

"Now, look what you've gone and done! There'll be no turning back now..."

"Wouldn't have it any other way..."

"A smart Lassie. I love ya' the more for it!"

"And I, you!"

They broke into laughter as the game drew to a close. Jimmy kissed her, marveling that he only loved her more as they moved into each future Now.

"If you're laughing,
it's Love."

192 JJ'S SHIP

"All things work together...
as they should."

It had always fascinated Jimmy that Nature worked so well, healing its own mistakes, birthing new great notions to replace that which had passed, flowing in some immense cyclical way through days and nights, seasons and years, employing all the great parts like gravity and momentum, and inertia. As a human fellow subject to the "laws of nature," he marveled at how much there seemed to be that still hadn't been figured out! Yet, Nature did it, well... naturally.

The marvel that was the human body was its science, the amazing machinations that signaled each other when to move and what to do, all listening somehow to the commands of the brain, the mind, the intention, there. It, too, could heal itself as if by magical means. In spite of the mind sometimes. Layers of skin and creativity are built to maintain the "temple of consciousness." Most ran autonomously, and thank god for that, as tinkering humans would have made a Frankenstein of things.

And the Mind, the elusive light of life, somehow residing in the uppermost part of the body, the head of the class, the ultimate guide through a life of miracles and the mundane, perceiving and discerning, judging and naming, thinking all the while that it was somehow in charge, when most everything ran on its own, without any "help," whatsoever. Egocentric and arrogant, craving acceptance and purpose and never satisfying either, forced to be content with the illusion of control while knowing that it was both inept and inferior in a world far superior to even imagination, left in awe and wonder, blundering in a world of its own making, cursing both luck and circumstance, when it generated both. And the only path through was something as ephemeral and misunderstood as Love.

Many a book the Mind has written, and all the sciences have attempted to comprehend and failed, while even the poets could not put a pin in the tale of it. Love. That which the Mind craved, and the body braved, pretending that there was a center, a heart, that was somehow separate from the Mind and perhaps more powerful. Incomprehensible yet simple. The "One Thing" that superseded everything else. Love that held no grudge, that didn't judge, that knew no hurt, did not project, that pointed ever towards Joy and acceptance, with its magical discernment and sense of humor, that recognized all music and natural flow and joined in it. Love.

And Jimmy loved it. He had given himself over to it repeatedly, his own religion of both purpose and reincarnation. He had been birthed in it and carried by it, a basket in the Nile River waiting to be found, reaching for a friendly breast and the sounds of Love.

And then, Jenny.

Once again, the miracle unfolded in his mind and body, his spirit fed by the idea of Love, his mind enthralled by it, and his body gave its all for it. It was all-encompassing, and there was no turning back. No understanding was required, just a little willingness. Finally, he had said "yes" to the All of It, and that had made all the difference.

"Jenny." He said her name as if it represented all the secrets of the Universe, which indeed it did. "Jenny, do you think we'll ever understand how we came to be together in this place at this time?" "Ah, Jimmy, my Thinker, Writer, Poet. Maybe we're not meant to understand it, and we're only meant to live it. Can that be enough for you?"
"I suppose so, Jenny. All things work together, don't they?"
"And in this case, not just for the good, but for the best!"
"It's just you and me in all the world, isn't it," Jimmy said as a matter of fact. "Everybody's running around in their little universes,

just like us, choosing how they want to feel and be and do. And somehow, it all works."

"And somehow, it all works really well." Jenny sighed and continued, touching his arm as she talked. "However, this mystery really works out. Let's just enjoy the part we're living right now."

Jimmy turned to look into Jenny's eyes to see once again the depth of acceptance there. "You know it, Jenny. And you know me better than anyone ever has before."

"Maybe that's because you've been so completely open, holding nothing back." She said it easily as if it were true.

Jimmy fell into his pirate brogue: "Ah, so it's up to me, is it? Well then, you'll be walking the plank a long time, Girlie!"

"Aye, and you'll be walking it with me, Captain!"

They laughed and fell into each other, holding tightly in the moment and releasing the very pulse of the Universe.

"I think I love you, Darling One."

"Normally, you think too much, but this time it's just right, Boyfriend!"

"Aye, that it is!"

"The ship awaits her Captain and his 1st Mate,
and the sails fill with the light of dawn."

193 JJ'S NOTE

"Music is the background
of all of life."

Jimmy enjoyed most of the music that reached his ears. He did avoid most country-western, rap, and metal, however, as they didn't resonate with his presumed taste in music. He liked what he liked. He didn't like what he didn't like. It didn't make One good and One bad - it remained a preference in the dream, and that is all. It didn't matter that the mind wanted to judge. It was always doing that.

Although some songs seemed to be associated with certain events - celebration lyrics, love lost, and love gained being some common themes - mostly, it was how a lyric fit a situation that brought a certain song to mind. "I want to fly like an eagle..." came from a feeling of exhilaration, not from a desire to go anywhere. "Desperado" was a love song. "You better shape up" had less to do with Grease than it did with acknowledging the joy of connection.

Jimmy had some song or another running in the background of his thinking mind most of the time. Sometimes, he hummed.

Jenny was like Jimmy in that she always seemed to have a song playing in the background, and she almost always was grinning. Music expressed the feelings that she carried and seemed to be evoked to match them. "Take it Easy" flowed into "Every Breath You Take" as easily and effortlessly as "Ob-La-Di, Ob-La-Da" became "All You Need is Love."

Love songs seemed the most prevalent, matching how Jenny

viewed the world. She loved life, and it loved her back. Hence the prevalent grin!

When Jimmy and Jenny danced, something amazing happened - the music seemed to vibrate all around them and through them. Sometimes, they couldn't tell if the music made them dance or if their dancing evoked the music. They were both synchronous and a source of sustenance - as if the dance fed the spirit, and the spirit fed the dance, hungry for communion.

Nearly every morning, they sang some snatches of song to one another. "Do you believe in magic?" Or maybe, "Back to the days of Christopher Robin..." Often, the joy of waking up together was enough to get them singing, like birds greeting the sun.

"Jenny." The sound of her name resonated with the vibration of love that he always felt around her." Jenny, do you think that a lot of what we say comes from song lyrics?"

"If 'I could save Time in a Bottle,' Jimmy, I might be able to tell you 'Just how much I Love You.'"

"Hahahaha! 'I want to be loved by you, by you and nobody else but you!'"

"A-lo-oo-one." They sang the last note together.

"Really, though, I think there is some truth in it."

"That we are always singing? 'Dream until your dream comes true,' Jimmy."

"'Oops, you did it again,' Jenny."

"I guess you'd say, 'What can make me feel this way...'"

"My Girl..."

"My Boy..."

"Love is All You Need."

"Open the door and let 'em in."

"Oh, what a beautiful morning..."

"Ev'ry-thing's going our way."

"Follow the Music."

194 JJ'S MOMENT

"In this moment,
One Love is All that's spoken."

Jimmy had been a bit slow learning the simple secret to life - that it's not in the getting so much as it's in the imagination, and life isn't a puzzle or even a thing - it's all a grand dream.

In the dream, everything imagined is as real as it gets. We follow our own breadcrumbs tossed out in front of us. Walking the path is not a balancing act unless we dream it as some tight wire defined by our past thoughts when it ought to be as wide as the sky and just as open to the sun.

Jimmy forgot this often. He could only golf as well as he allowed himself to play; he weighed what he thought he should weigh, and he loved exactly how he had taught himself to love.

Now, there was no turning back. Love, realized, changed everything. "All in" meant just that. What at first looked like a lifeline became an all-prevailing sense of wonder, and he rode the wave of it, her by his side, like two pro surfers syncing with the dance of the ocean.

Jenny.

She had come to represent this Great Love in the dream. Like the Muse in some grand myth, Jenny had called to him, and he had answered, braving the rocky shores to find Love in her arms and lightning in her eyes.

The wandering was over. The wondering had just begun.

"Jenny." Her very name called to him from some deep place, now, from the new-found depths that she had taken him. "Jenny, you still amaze me!"

"Of course I do. You dreamed it that way!"

"See, there, you did it again. When we are present with each other, it's like we are of One Mind, playing along with Itself."

"And no one is winning! Or losing, for that matter."

Jimmy laughed with her, relishing the interplay, the magic, the Love in the exchange. "I'm the luckiest man alive."

"Well, that's a given, considering you are the only man that you'll ever know..."

"Ha! See what I mean! And relentless at that."

"As you like it," Jenny responded coyly. "There's only One of us here, so you're really having this conversation with yourself."

"No wonder it's so brilliant."

"Isn't it, Jimmy?"

"It's just how we both like it."

"Simultaneous orgasm?"

"Is there any other kind, really, Jenny?"

"So, we make love to ourselves..." her voice trailed off, and he picked up the notion.

"... in the shadow of the world." His voice ended in a whisper as if this great truth held all the libraries of the field of thought. He leaned in to kiss her, softly at first, then deeper as he gave himself to the moment and her.

> *"Dream for the laughter.*
> *Skip the tears."*

195 JJ'S WISH

"Prayer is acknowledging
that One is One with All."

Jimmy never prayed anymore. At least not the way he was taught as a child or abandoned as an unrequited teen. Not even when the first person that he really knew passed over. Jimmy had decided that he was enough, all on his own, and that seemed to be all he ever really had, any time anyway. Prayer was for kids.

Meditation was different in that nothing was asked for, the Mind simply attempted to get out of the way to quit influencing everything. Jimmy often drifted completely away when he tried to meditate. He couldn't remember any significant images or symbols to give meaning to the experience or to justify the time spent doing nothing. And he didn't really get answers, either.

He got answers when he suspended thinking for a moment or two and sent out a flare of questioning intention, expecting an answer. He thought to himself: 'I am looking into a future that may or may not have happened to see what did happen.' It was a strange thought, like knowing that déjà vu came from remembering dreams that he once had. But it was his preferred method for making decisions or perhaps justifying them. If he could perceive only what he thought he could, then he had already answered any questions for himself.

The idea of "Present Moment Awareness" tickled his Mind, so he took it in, gave it some space, and enjoyed the heightened perceptual field that it inspired. In that field Rumi wrote about, "I'll meet you there," Jimmy sensed a Oneness with what he perceived and how he was living, an acceptance of what seemed to be arising on its own but might also be arising from his intentions both conscious and unconscious, or semi-conscious. Whatever was going on.

The "Whatever was going on" didn't seem to include the gods of his childhood or the prayers that went with those concepts. Some sort of "acceptance" replaced the ideas of "wanting" or "needing."

"Desire" seemed a much simpler thing to manage and worked well with the newer ideas of resonance and vibration that the Mind had conjured up to keep "him" entertained. The Universe "matching his vibration" seemed a little like "wanting something to happen a certain way," so Jimmy withheld a little belief even if that was also being responded to... It was a "Self" preservation tactic, obviously. But at least there was no prompting to "pray" for anything, even if the "what" didn't always match the "why." Wasn't the "how" all that mattered? Didn't the "Now" supersede all of it? "Present Moment Awareness" was Jimmy's new god, being that he seemed to rise above his egoic self to "know without knowing" that he was "One with everything." It felt like that, anyway, at least for a moment. Now and Then, being relative.

Jimmy had not expected Jenny to show up in his life. He hadn't "seen" her coming in his projected future, and he hadn't prayed about it, either. Sure, he had casually tossed out an idea into the Universe that he might "like someone to talk to" since the house was colder and quieter after the dog died. Maybe the response from the Universe went deeper than he knew, presently, to buried desires for amazing love like the fairy tales of childhood or the stuff of dreams. Jimmy didn't know, and Jimmy didn't care to know. In his "Present Moment Awareness," he was just enjoying the show and the great joy of "Living in the Now" with Love preoccupying his thought systems.

Love was easy. Jenny was amazing. Life was very, very good. If Jimmy prayed at all, it was that this would never end.

"Jenny." Jimmy always felt it when he spoke her name or even thought of the love that they shared - that everything was perfect with the world. "Jenny, it does look like everything is unfolding for our greatest good, doesn't it?"

"Jimmy, you know it." Jenny knew that she knew it, too - that the Universe had somehow brought them together to increase the recognition of Love in the world, to bring "real-ization" to the expression of It, to somehow "show by example" the Joy that was possible, that was still possible in this "shattering of dreams in the world of perception." She knew that Jimmy knew it, all right. He was the same reflection of her that she was for him and that recognition was everything.

Love reflected Love.

"Jenny, you know it, too! And that does make all the difference!" Jimmy's excitement was now "the norm," as if the joy of love had flipped a switch that said, "See only Love!"

"I love it when you talk reality, Boyfriend!"

"Only Love is real, Girlfriend!"

"That's what I'm talkin' about!"

"It Is What It Is!"

"And that's a lot!" They burst into laughter as the joy of exchange became more than their grins could describe.

"I love this, whatever it is."

"It's Love, Jimmy, and I love it, too. Let's keep on doing it, K?"

"That sounds like an invitation!"

"It was supposed to, Boy."

"I gladly accept!" Jimmy embraced her and everything that she represented so well: love, woman, mate, friend, lover, Muse, mirror.

Joy had answered all of his "prayers."

"Be careless
what you wish for."

196 JJ'S REPEAT

*"The dream is
always about Love."*

It was hard for Jimmy to remember how it once felt when he was
alone in the world. He'd spent most of his life trying to avoid the
realization that perception was a very solitary thing - no two persons
seeing alike - if there were any other persons at all - from the Mind's
viewpoint, he could barely prove that even he existed.

Love seemed to involve "others," and as such, it was probably the
only thing that saved him from a lonely existence. So, Jimmy looked
for love anywhere and everywhere until he gave up, exhausted from
the search, content to live out a semi-interesting existence chasing the
whims of the mind.

Then Jenny.

Even Jenny didn't seem real at first, showing up unexpectedly and
professing love so quickly. Unprepared for love, Jimmy pushed it
away, not daring to embrace the very feelings that he had ultimately
given up on as only leading to heartache and country-western songs.

Then, the universe changed the storyline. People were
disappearing and making time seem so real. And in a previous
moment of forever, Jimmy had said, "I'm All In." And that changed
everything.

"Jenny." Jimmy's heart touched the idea of Love every time he
spoke her name. And it felt sublime and wonderful. "Jenny, do you

think we really have any control over what's going on?"

"Ah, Jimmy. We can't know anything for sure, can we? But it seems, at times, that we at least choose how we feel about what shows up..."

"I feel like that's true!" Jimmy laughed and went on. "I know I chose to be 'All In,' or it felt like a choice because everything changed after that. Now, I don't live alone. We live as One as we can get, always returning to love each other again and again, and it's the best life ever. And I DO hope that I had at least a Pinky finger in it!"

Jenny laughed, too. "More than just your Pinky, Boyfriend! You're 'All In', and so am I. And that is greater than either of us ever knew it could be."

"And the world reflects that, doesn't it!" Jimmy spoke excitedly now. "And it seems that people around us notice the flow or something. It's weird, but it sort of makes it feel even more real, knowing that others can see it in us!"

"It does, doesn't it, Jimmy?" Jenny grinned, as usual. "It's fun to see the world reflect our love for each other, but it keeps coming back to this moment, where we choose over and over to love without holding anything back. This Now. I look into your eyes, and that's the only thing that's real."

Jimmy looked deeply into her sparkling eyes, mesmerized by the light he saw there and knowing without words that it reflected his own light. "It's the only thing that's real." He repeated. "Everything else is just context."

"A fun place to play!"

Jimmy broke from his reverie. He couldn't resist the urge to tickle Jenny's side. Maybe it was proof that she was real if she reacted to his touch. "Goddess, I love you!"

Jenny squirmed and laughed under his fingers. "I love you, too, Boy."

And that was all that ever mattered, Now.

"Choose 'happy' in the dream.
Repeatedly."

197 JJ'S MEMORY

"Memories change with time and perspective.
What's seen Now is the only Truth."

Jimmy knew that Jenny had brought a new perspective into his life - that Love was real, and everything else was imagined. "Reality" was an experience made from the merging of ideas about what was seen, heard, and, most importantly, felt. Feelings were everything that touched: hands, hearts, thoughts, songs, memories, worlds. Their Venn Diagram had many concentric circles, Now, though "past experiences" lay mainly outside the circle. In 3D, their futures spiraled out together like a "time jump" effect in a movie. They would go together and land, hand in hand, to stare out on new horizons.

The house was almost empty now. They had packed memories neatly in boxes and taped them tightly - they were making new memories now, and the old ones had become relics to look back upon and wonder who they had really been. Each had come so far - to know things so differently, then - to know the world the same now in this moment. The new miracles were stacked upon the memories of the old, stepping stones to see the new world.

"Jenny." Jimmy considered her presence in his life as a major miracle and spoke her name as if this were true. "Jenny, do you think history repeats itself, or is it just the mind being lazy?"
Jenny considered the question a moment or two. Jimmy had a way of thinking that intrigued her mind, too, as if everything was a new

puzzle to figure out - start with the borders and fill in the scenes. She knew that her history had changed as she had changed. It wasn't possible to see the world with the eyes of the past, so it was impossible to repeat it exactly, but what of the dreams that remained the same? "Jimmy, I think the Mind uses characters from the dreams of the past to create the dream of the present. Context, you know. If it were completely different, the Mind would go bonkers."

"Too late for me, then, you say?" Jimmy laughed at himself. He had learned that this was a great way to connect with others without offending them. Jimmy had found out that how everyone saw the world was colored by their past mistakes, hoping not to repeat them, listening for clues to pick a path through the rubble of shattered dreams. Jimmy laughed at himself, too, to keep his ego slightly off balance so it wouldn't think too highly of itself to the exclusion of what 'his-self' was feeling at this moment.

"Jenny, I think you're right! The Universe uses the same characters not because it's run out of ideas but because we feel at home considering new ones! You're a genius!"

"Glad you finally noticed, Jimmy!" Jenny laughed with him. It was part of her "job description" as a best friend to poke fun and to keep his ego in check. She enjoyed doing that well. "I'd say the same for you if I could." They both laughed at that.

"I'm glad the Universe used all the best parts of my ideas of 'friend' and 'lover' when It made you up, Girlfriend!"

"Fairy tales do come true, Jimmy!" Even her eyes were grinning now.

"And we'll live happily ever after?"

"That's how I see it, Boyfriend!"

"Then it must be true! 'Cause that's how I see it, too!"

"We dream well together, don't we?" Jenny said it as a fact, not a question.

"It's a dreamy dream. And I wouldn't want it any other way. I've proved that enough times already."

"Ah, Jimmy. Everything we lived in the past brought us to this moment. We wouldn't have connected in this way without the similar dreams in the past."

"That's true, Jenny. All those ragged edges that fit together like pieces of an intricate puzzle..." His voice drifted off dreamily.

"And we get to make up the new scene in the middle!" Jenny said it excitedly. "Are you ready?"

"I'm always ready for you, Girlfriend. I was born ready, as a matter of fact!"

"Well, then!" Jenny laughed. "Let's go!"

"Sharing dreams is essential
to a successful relationship.
It's how Love expresses."

198 JJ'S TURN

"The will of god will never lead you
where the grace of god cannot keep you."

Jimmy had heard it all before. "God will never give you more than you can handle." He had managed to make it through a few times when it looked like he'd had more than he could handle, but it had been more like survival instinct than anything to do with faith in some unapproachable "god." Jimmy had learned something that he could use when things got a little dark: "Follow the prompting toward love." This made any decision a lot simpler. Love meant Joy. For Jimmy, this meant: "If it makes you happy, do it." Simple. To the point. Knowable. No faith was required.

Life was a complete mystery, anyway. He really had no idea how he had ended up where he had ended up. Again and again, he would pause and wonder WTH and just shake his head. And things seemed to turn out OK if he just allowed that "Wherever he was, there he was." And that was that. Every day rolled out pretty much the same as the one before, only there were small differences that evidently added up to big ones, as he could recall not even living in this same house before, and now it seemed that he would be leaving it for some new place. "It's the little things." That's another aphorism that Jimmy could live with. It matched his experience.

Then there was Jenny.

Talk about not knowing what had happened - this would be number one on the list of "Everything happens for the good." Jimmy was pretty sure there was a Bible quote for that one, although he seemed to recall that "that other guy" - Krishna, he thought - said much the same thing. Which had come first? It didn't matter. What did matter was that Jenny was now intricate to his life, his joy, his "heading" in life. And he knew that she hadn't been here before. He was so glad that she was here, now. Talk about "Following your joy!"

Love had been a slippery thing for Jimmy. He thought he had found it more than once, and maybe he had, for a while. He wasn't sure what had happened. But here he was, "in love" for the very first time, or something like that "first time" when the stars are brighter, and the moon is the favorite light when love songs all make sense, and everything is sort of funny because you're so happy anyway. And here he was, feeling love and speaking love and knowing love like he never had before! And every little thing was wonderful.

Little things kept shifting the world a bit at a time, but "in this time," love was going to rule it all. In this Now, Jenny was everything he had ever imagined love could be and then some. Amazingly, dreams could come true even when you weren't looking! Now, Jimmy said, "If there is a god - thank you, thank you, thank you."

Jenny and Jimmy seemed to dream alike, at least in the "waking part," where they could compare notes. Together, they followed the promptings toward Joy, and life kept turning out really good. Love was their god, and Jenny was the Goddess! Jimmy, continuously amazed at how life was turning up, had become adept at following the Joy. Joy was whatever made Jenny smile at him, and she smiled a lot! And even though Jenny lived her own life, working her job, remembering her different pasts, the two of them were dreaming up life together now. And it was good.

"Jenny." Jimmy laughed as he spoke her name, feeling the joy that he associated with everything that had her mark on it - and that was almost everything now. "Jenny, Jenny, Jenny. You know that saying about real estate values?"

"That the three most important things to look for are 'location, location, location?' Yup. I know that one!"

"Well, in my life, it's now 'you, you, you!'"

"Ah, Jimmy. You do inspire me!"

"Ditto, Girlfriend. You make me feel good about being myself, and that's probably the number one thing that makes me so happy."

"Ditto back atcha, Boyfriend! That and a quarter will get us a cup of coffee. I hope so, that is. I don't have a quarter on me, though."

"You still get coffee!"

"Yay! Just what I always wanted!"

"Only we didn't even believe it! And now it's like we're in our own world, and that's all that matters. That and whatever we're going to do today!"

"And the only thing that matters is what we do together!"

"That sums it up. And I'm looking forward to seeing what that is!"

"Well, it's going to be good, that much is for sure."

"Love colors everything."

199 JJ'S FLOW

"The ocean supports the body,
allowing it to float.
Struggling makes it sink."

Jimmy was glad that he had learned to swim as a youth. Moving through water felt like "smooth sailing," as if life was something you pulled in by the handful to propel yourself forward through time. Sometimes, he swam hard; sometimes, he merely sculled along, gazing up at the sky, which barely moved, which didn't move except for the illusion of clouds passing by. Maybe he was in a "Truman Show" of his own making?

Thank goodness that Jenny had shown up when she did! Jenny was a swimmer, too, having crossed an ocean of her own to cruise at his side. Now, the dream moved together as if the energy of their joined intentions was enough to move the world, at least a little. Or maybe it was a shared vision of "how things were" and how they might be, and the dream was like a time machine, transporting them on a carpet made of whimsy.

At least they moved together, sharing the commentary, watching for the anomalies as if looking for clues to what made the flow go...

And they flowed together.

"Going with the Flow
is the only way to know."

200 JJ'S BANTER

"It's a reflection that we see.
Always, you're a part of me."

Jimmy had a good memory. 'Too good, sometimes,' he thought. 'There are things I'd rather forget.'

He had also learned along the way that none of those thoughts (and memories) determined who or how he might "be" in the world. Every day was a fresh one. Every hour, a new sun. Every moment, life was undone. And then, a chance to start again!

Forgiveness is forgetfulness.

All Jimmy really wanted was to relax into life a little more and share everything with Jenny. The numbers and equations could work themselves out with minimal, if any, effort. 'There is definitely a flow to things,' he thought and held on to the idea as he had for most of his life. 'And I want to ride that wave.'

Life had certainly surprised him as he lived it and learned to love it. Jenny had been one of the biggest surprises! (Even though she was little.)

The lyrics "Five foot two, eyes of blue, walk across your swimming pool" seemed to fit Jenny perfectly. 'My Goddess,' Jimmy thought and tried to treat her as such, always. He changed the Sugartime lyrics to - "Coffee in the morning, walking in the evening, dinner at supper time..." Jenny was sweet as sugar and flavored Jimmy's life with her presence. Life had become an adventure again! Jimmy "looked on the world with soft eyes," and love was everywhere he looked. Jenny had opened him up to love again, and

Jimmy had gone "All in." Together, life unfolded in new ways for both of them. Love had them riding tandem towards an unknown future, and it was exquisite fun!

"Jenny!" Jimmy called to her gleefully. "The rabbits are out to say 'hi' again!" It seemed that they really did show up when they looked for them. Sort of like Love.

"I think they love you, Boyfriend!"

"Well, if they do, it's because of you!"

"Little Ol' Me?" Jenny spoke coquettishly.

"Yes, Little Ol' You! I was content to hide in my hole, and then... Well, then I gave you a drawer, and that changed everything!"

"Give a girl an inch..." Jenny grinned.

"Like taking in a stray cat." Jimmy ignored the innuendo, at least for the moment.

"You want me to leave?"

"Never, Darling. Life has never been this good. I wouldn't change a thing. Except for when I got mustard on my shirt or when I knocked over the coffee cup on the bed stand."

"Everything good's a little messy," Jenny philosophized.

"And there's always a shower or a paper towel around to help clean up!"

"Life is about Love.
It's a simple equation."

Books by Brian Logsdon

100 Days of JJ – A Unique Love Story, Book 1

100 Days of JJ – A Unique Love Story, Book 2

100 Days of JJ – A Unique Love Story, Book 3

100 Days of JJ – A Unique Love Story, Book 4

Lifelines: Chronicle of a Time-Traveling Wizard

Vortex: A Journey of Awakening to Self

ABOUT THE AUTHOR

Brian Logsdon met Lori Cereck the same way that Jimmy met Jenny – on the dance floor!

Brian first learned to waltz with a favorite nun at St. Peter's Grade School and then found solace in western swing dancing, disco, and his all-time favorite – the slow dance!

Brian is continually awakened at 3:11 a.m. with the urge to write. Lori allows him the space to do just that. And also offers inspiration! The two lead a rather inseparable life, traveling whenever possible and dreaming of all the places they will go!